D1421199

About the Author

Bogdan B. Rusev is a Bulgarian writer of genre-subversive fiction. He was the editor-in-chief of several magazines and the creative director of two advertising agencies before he turned to full-time writing and translating modern fiction. This is his first novel to be published in the UK. He lives in Sofia with his wife and cat.

To Z.

Bogdan B. Rusev

A Tourist,
He Thought

AUSTIN MACAULEY
PUBLISHERS LTD.

Copyright © Bogdan B. Rusev (2016)

The right of Bogdan B. Rusev to be identified as author of this work has been asserted by him in accordance with section 77 and 78 of the Copyright, Designs and Patents Act 1988.

All rights reserved. No part of this publication may be reproduced, stored in a retrieval system, or transmitted in any form or by any means, electronic, mechanical, photocopying, recording, or otherwise, without the prior permission of the publishers.

Any person who commits any unauthorized act in relation to this publication may be liable to criminal prosecution and civil claims for damages.

A CIP catalogue record for this title is available from the British Library.

ISBN 978 1 78455 817 8 (paperback)
      978 1 78455 818 5 (hardback)
      978 1 78455 819 2 (eBook)

www.austinmacauley.com

First Published (2016)
Austin Macauley Publishers Ltd.
25 Canada Square
Canary Wharf
London
E14 5LQ

Printed and bound in Great Britain

1. Prague

The tourist hated Prague. He had been several times and every time the weather had been disgusting; he did not know when they were shooting all the photographs for postcards, airlines' complimentary magazines and hotel reservation websites on which one could see "Golden Prague" with the deep rich colours of the rooftops and the sky. When he arrived, the sky was the usual grey. It was raining, cold and unpleasant. The tourist took a taxi from the airport and gave the driver a page torn from his notebook on which he had written the name and address of the hotel, as he did not trust himself to pronounce them correctly.

During the drive, the tourist was looking outside through the window, but he did not see anything good. On the opposite side of the street from the hotel entrance, there was a broad stone staircase dotted with bronze statues. The statues were facing the hotel, accusingly.

The tourist checked in, left his only travel bag in his room and went outside again. It kept drizzling.

The famous bridge with the statues was undergoing a renovation. Half of it was under scaffolding, with clear plastic on top. Behind the plastic, one could see workers fixing the pavement or smoking cigarettes. There were crowds surrounding all the remaining statues, trying to photograph themselves without including the other people in the shot. One of the statues was evidently more interesting than the others; there even more people surrounding it, waiting in line to take a photograph, stamping their feet and breathing on their hands in the cold.

Following the signs, the tourist found the bottom station of a funicular and used it to reach the top of a hill. One could see the next hill from the top, with the historical quarter of Prague and the castle and all the rest, but the tourist had already visited them and did not want to go again. Instead, he followed a path through the grey forest, under the heavy cold raindrops leaking from the trees, and reached a small metal structure that looked like a scaled down version of the Eiffel Tower. There was a wet lawn in front and people of all ages were absorbed in some kind of game. They were playing in couples and using marbles; the tourist had never seen this game before and paused to watch them, but he did not know the rules and quickly lost interest. He did not want to go back the same route, so he walked down the steep paths and chanced upon a small, rundown house in the forest, operating as a gallery. He paid the entrance fee to a girl who did not speak anything else but Czech and entered.

The gallery was exceptionally cramped, consisting of several floors of a single room each, linked with a creaking spiral staircase. All the walls, including those of the staircase, were densely covered with oil paintings. All the paintings were by the same artist who loved his fiery reds, deep purples, bright oranges and the like. The artist himself could be seen on nearly all the paintings, as the facial features of all the male characters were the same. The features of all the female characters were the same, too, so the model for them must have been the artist's wife. The subjects were fairytale stuff: for example, the artist's wife, in the form of a woodland spirit, was sleeping in a huge blossom as the artist himself, in the form of an improbably muscled centaur, was watching her, enthralled. The titles of the paintings were strange as well and the tourist copied some of them in his notebook. There was coffee and tea for the visitors on the ground floor of the gallery, as well as a thick file of newspaper clippings showing the artist – in real life – meeting other artists and politicians.

The tourist went out of the gallery and walked back to his hotel. He had a cold. He found a pharmacy on the corner and bought himself some cold pills, then he found another shop staffed exclusively by Vietnamese people and bought himself a bottle of absinthe. He went up to his room, took a hot shower, changed and swallowed the pills. Then he poured some absinthe in the toothbrush glass from the bathroom and drank it with no ice and no special preparation. Consumed in this manner, absinthe was just ordinary alcohol, admittedly quite strong.

The tourist opened his notebook and very carefully examined his room, noting down some things. The room was ordinary. Thinking about what he could possibly write about this hotel, he drank two more glasses of absinthe and the perspective of getting dressed and going out again to have dinner started to seem completely unacceptable. He brushed his teeth and went to bed.

He woke up several hours later, unreasonably early in local time. The idea for the hotel review had come in the night, as it often did. He opened his laptop and wrote the story in the voice of a clever imaginary character – a private detective with eccentric habits and irresistible charisma – who travelled the world hunting for traces of the existence of some sort of fairy-tale creatures; the tourist pictured them like the wife of the artist from the small gallery in the forest, although he did not provide a description. Needless to say, Prague was one of hunting grounds that the fantastic detective frequented most often, and he always stayed in this hotel because of its proximity to several spots in the city which were the location of repeated inexplicable phenomena. The facts about the hotel – address, number of rooms, etc. – were discreetly embedded in the story of the fairytale creature hunter.

The tourist read his review one more time and decided that it was quite acceptable. He wrote a hotel review once every couple of days and was very rarely wrong in his judgement. He connected to the tourist website that he worked freelance for, and used his password to send in the new review. His editor would read it later and then upload it on the website where the users would be able to rate and comment on it. On the same day or the next one at most, the tourist would receive his fee in his international bank card account, with the option for a bonus if the review brought a certain number of unique visits to the tourist website. The cost of the tourist's stay in the hotel would be covered by his employers as well, but there was a separate department which managed barter deals and he was not completely sure how this worked.

The tourist opened the section for orders which listed all the other hotels which had already signed a contract with the tourist website and were waiting for a review writer to visit them. He had to go on to Vienna which was not much of a challenge as there were eight hotels in Vienna on the waiting list. The tourist made a reservation, exited his profile and cut the connection. It was already eight in the morning and he went down to the hotel restaurant to have breakfast.

The only other people in the hotel restaurant were a young couple. They were looking at a map and a travel guide in English but they were speaking some Slavic language. The woman was in her late twenties. The man was in his early thirties but he had one of those boyish faces which are very good at concealing real age. He was wearing quality sports brands and hiking boots fit to climb a mountain peak. There was just fruit on the woman's plate; his plate had the remains of a high-protein breakfast on it.

The tourist took some scrambled eggs and toast. Then he sat down several tables away from the couple, who smiled at him. He smiled back and started eating. They continued talking in their language and their voices and body language suggested that they had resumed the discussion of their plans for the day.

The tourist had a notion about their plans for the day. Like him, they had arrived in Prague yesterday, albeit on a different flight. They had checked in the hotel and then they had used the afternoon to see the modern part of the city, leaving the more interesting old part for the second day when they would have more time to see it.

The windows of the restaurant looked on the staircase with the bronze statues and one could also see a little sky. The sky was less grey than it was yesterday. Perhaps there would be some sunshine later and the couple would be able to take some photographs of the kind that presented Prague in a better light.

The tourist did not plan to go out. After the couple left the restaurant (the man said goodbye in English and the woman just nodded with an absentminded smile), he stood up and poured himself a cup of coffee, even though he had a nervous stomach and tried to keep off caffeine in the morning.

His stomach was up in arms even before he could finish the coffee. He went up to his room to use the toilet, almost running over the last couple of steps.

2. Vienna

The tourist did not like luggage. Everything that he needed fitted in a middle-sized travel bag, no wheels, which, in turn, fitted in the overhead luggage compartment on the plane. In the bag, he carried a minimal amount of clothes in neutral colours which he sent out for washing in hotels or simply threw away when he bought new ones; the few toiletries one was allowed to take on a plane; the black laptop he used for work; and one or two paperbacks which he bought from airport bookstores (usually chosen with an eye for the price-volume ratio rather than the name of the author) and then forgot on purpose in his hotel room or by the pool. The tourist had no personal effects. If something happened to his luggage, he was able to recover everything in a single day, including the files in his computer which he copied to his e-mail account.

He took a taxi to the station and boarded the international express train which passed through Bratislava. For some strange reason, the dining car served Hungarian meals and the tourist lunched on goulash and a small bottle of white wine. The tracks passed through a series of long tunnels and climbed the mountains in a series of sharp turns, and when they stopped in Brno, one could see some of the old city and the castle on the hill above the station, but the weather had turned even colder and more unpleasant.

Bratislava was like a smaller Prague – with a miniature old city and a river straddled by a bridge with an anachronistically modern construction – and it was terribly cold. The tourist spent several hours aimlessly walking the city, entering shops, selecting a souvenir and holding it for a while, then leaving it back where he had found it and walking out.

The first time he met the young couple from the hotel restaurant in Prague, they were walking out of a gift shop and the woman looked at him for a moment as if she was about to recognise him, but then the man said something and pointed at the things that they had bought – toilet- and bathroom-door signs with colourful pictures of a little girl taking a bath and a little boy taking a piss – the woman started laughing and she was still laughing and looking into the man's eyes as they passed.

The second time the tourist was sitting in a café, drinking black tea and cognac and waiting to get warm. He had bought leather gloves from a shop on the main street but his fingers were still frozen. The man and the woman entered the same café and sat by the window. After they ordered and watched the street outside for a while, the man looked inside and saw him. Then he did something that made the tourist go stiff for a moment: he stood up, approached him, said hello and asked him to sit at their table. The tourist stood up awkwardly and followed the man to the window. The man reminded the woman that they had been in the same hotel in Prague, she smiled and nodded. Then the man introduced them and the tourist joined them at their table.

The man and the woman were very nice. They told him that they were on a pre-honeymoon of sorts, as they planned to get married in several months and they thought that after the wedding, they would have neither the money nor the time to travel. The tourist guessed that the woman was pregnant; instead he made the joke that they clearly took their weddings seriously where they came from. When they asked him what he did for a living, he told them the truth. As usual, they reacted with amicable envy. Most people had to work for a year to be able to stay in a good hotel in an interesting place, while it was the tourist's job to stay in good hotels in interesting places. As usual, the tourist did not try to disprove this. When they asked him about his next destination, he was vague. The young couple were to go on to Vienna where they would board a flight to Havana. The tourist had another cognac at their table, then he wished them a pleasant journey and left.

Bratislava and Vienna were ridiculously close to each other. A ship left the Danube port every hour; a bus left the station every thirty minutes. The tourist chose the bus and had a short, boring trip on the highway.

In Vienna, it was even colder. The streets were wide, the buildings were tall and tomb-like and an icy wind screamed between them. The tourist had printed a map on the black-and-white hotel printer in Prague and decided to walk but he was frozen once again by the time he got there. His face was burning and his hands and feet were raw. The sky above the city was clear and there were people in pullovers on the streets, enjoying the spring sun. The tourist thought that this was absurd.

His hotel was named after a German composer and the street was named after a Hungarian composer. At least none of them was named after Mozart.

The tourist left his bag in the room, put on all the clothes that he owned and went out again. The wind had died down and some of the people he walked by were in short sleeves.

The city seemed to consist entirely of shopping streets and pedestrian zones, both crowded. The big cathedral in the centre of the city, where two pedestrian zones and several shopping streets converged, was undergoing reconstruction work and most of it was covered with scaffolding, covered in turn by a depiction of the cathedral underneath – just like every other famous cathedral the tourist had ever seen.

On the way back, the tourist was stopped in the street by a young woman pushing a pram. The woman seemed very pleasantly surprised to see him. It took him several seconds to place her: she was his first girlfriend in high school. The tourist thought that she looked better back then. She spoke with a German accent now. The baby was her sister's. The two of them had a short, increasingly clumsy conversation. The tourist could not think of a single thing to ask her. Her questions could be answered in monosyllables or even shrugs. After a few minutes, the two of them were relieved to part again and the tourist almost ran into a shoe store where he was certain to feel less awkward.

In spite of the temperature outside, they had the summer collections out. The shop assistants followed the man in the coat and the gloves who stopped at the sandals and flip-flops and asked him if he needed help. The tourist replied that he did not.

Clutching his purchase (blue flip-flops by a brand that he had seen advertised in magazines), he walked back to his hotel. In the lobby, next to the lifts, there was a shelf full of flyers. Most of them advertised tourist routes, open top buses, walking tours and the like, but at the back of the shelf were a dozen flyers featuring amateur naked photographs of different young women, phone numbers and multiple exclamation marks. The tourist looked around. There was no one else in the lobby and the receptionist was bent over the computer. The lift doors opened, the tourist grabbed several flyers and went in.

His room was narrow, the ceiling was high and there was central heating instead of air conditioning. The tourist turned the heat all the way up, took a hot shower and put his clothes back on. His throat already hurt so much that he was not sure if he would be able to talk. Sometimes several days passed without him having to talk to anyone, anyway.

He switched on his laptop and checked the websites of the prostitutes who had listed a website on their flyers. Most girls' photographs were too small and their faces were blurred. The tourist preferred the more old-fashioned censoring technique where they used thick black bands across their eyes. Finally, he chose a girl and e-mailed the website which offered her services.

The website replied almost immediately, as he was browsing the meagre contents of the minibar. The agency thanked him for his interest and informed him that the girl he had ordered would be in his hotel room from eight until nine in the evening, the whole operation completed with the exemplary discretion which had helped this particular agency rise to the top of the market. The tourist had heart palpitations and his stomach cramped. It was six fifteen. He used the toilet, then he had another hot shower and tried to relax on the bed where he drank several miniature bottles of whisky from the minibar. At six fifty he suddenly sat up, opened his laptop and e-mailed the same website to excuse himself that he had to cancel at the last minute, but he was actually on a business trip and he had just found out that the business meeting he was in was about to continue much longer than he had expected. He was not sure if it was not already too late for that, but a minute later the agency e-mailed back to assure him that it was not a problem at all, they were sorry that he had to work so late and they were hoping that he would contact them again next time he was in Vienna.

The tourist closed his laptop, relieved. Another miniature bottle of whisky and thirty minutes of local news on the television later, he thought that he might really work late. His fingers were still cold but the whisky had at least managed to numb the ache in his throat, and if he went outside now he was certain to see at least a couple of people in Bermuda shorts.

He opened a new file on his laptop and wrote a review for the hotel in which he claimed that the whole could be judged by its constituent parts – a kind of holographic theory of hotels for which he drew comparisons from classical music and architecture. He started with a detailed description of the stationery that he found in a desk drawer, measuring the distance between the hotel logo and the end of the page, and soon immersed himself in his work, getting up on several occasions to check, for example, the exact number of cotton buds sealed in a plastic bag in the toiletries basket in the bathroom, or the ratio between the lengths of the face towel and the body towel. When he was finished, he sent off the review, turned off the laptop and went to bed.

He woke up completely ill. His throat hurt so much that he winced every time he swallowed, he felt weak and he had a fever although he did not have a thermometer to prove it. He dressed and went down for breakfast in the hotel restaurant. The restaurant was underground, with tiny tables for two with white tablecloths. At every one of them sat a single man or a single woman, having breakfast (eggs and ham for the men, muesli and fruit for the women), reading financial newspapers and looking exactly like all the others. The tourist drank several glasses of orange juice and ate a croissant with butter. The restaurant speakers were playing Mozart.

They told him at reception that the station for the express train between the city centre and the airport was within walking distance. The tourist took his bag and walked. Some of the route was underground, along a protracted tunnel which seemed to host a single continuous supermarket. The tourist passed by Austrian men the kind of which he had not seen before, above ground: old men with long, graying blond hair and moustaches and bright blue, crazy eyes who walked like boxers and shoved into people on purpose.

In the express train, there were small displays which played the same infomercial about Vienna over and over. The tourist watched it in a stupor several times until the train arrived at the airport. He was not certain that he was leaving the same city. In the city that he was watching on the displays, there were singing fountains and children in shorts and flower dresses who were running and laughing, running and laughing, and the big cathedral in the centre was not covered with scaffolding.

The tourist checked in at the airport and passed through to the gate although he had two hours and thirty minutes before his flight was due to take off. Then he counted the coins in his pocket, bought a large hot coffee in a paper cup and dropped the remaining coins in a glass jar for some charity, careful not to see what the charity was. He just did not want to have European coins in his pocket when he arrived in Cuba because they would get mixed with the local coins.

The young couple from Prague and Bratislava was waiting at the gate for his flight. They were playing cards and when he nodded in greeting, they looked up at him in surprise. The man, in particular, seemed to be shocked, then he tensed and his face articulated faux delight. The woman was looking at him with something bordering on suspicion. The tourist thought that he should have told them about his next destination when he had met them in Bratislava.

Instead he told them that he had just received his latest order to review a hotel in Havana. The man laughed and said that they were about to stay in the same hotel. It must be their destiny to travel together. The woman did not look like she thought the same way but she did not say anything. The tourist wished them a pleasant flight and left them to their game, then he hid in a bookstore and stayed there until the boarding was called.

3. Havana

The tourist was immediately disgusted with Cuba and the Cubans as soon as he arrived in Havana and went for a walk along the large seaside boulevard. The too wide smiles on their faces which too often were sallow or pocked by unknown skin conditions; the shockingly loud laughter and shouting when they passed each other in large, aimless groups; the insufferable persistence when they chatted him up and tried to sell him their inevitable cigars, to bully him into giving them a present, or, more to the point, money.

The bottle of Dominican rum that he had bought in the free shop at the airport in Vienna was left in his room in the old hotel built by the U.S. mob in the nineteen twenties. The tourist turned his back on the darkening ocean, crossed the wide boulevard with its nonsensical Soviet automobiles and American gas guzzlers from the nineteen fifties, each one stuffed with eight Cubans, and followed a tree-lined alley between the ancient buildings with run-down facades which must have been beautiful a long time ago.

Immediately, an overweight woman about half his age approached him, asked him how he felt and what his name was, took his hand with her strong warm fingers and made him sit with her on a stone bench. When he replied in his uncertain Spanish, he suddenly found out that his throat did not hurt at all – his cold had disappeared in the hot wet Havana night. The woman was laughing and pressing her body against his and talking too quickly, repeating a word that the tourist suspected meant "modest" or even "cowardly". He asked her how much but she waved the question off and told him not to worry about it, then she stood up and took him by the hand along the horribly dirty alleys with scraggy dogs watching them curiously under the yellow light of the street lamps. They climbed the stinking staircase of a building that looked like it had been bombed, and the prostitute started banging on the door of a room at the bottom of the corridor, until finally the door was opened by a sleepy overweight young man, even younger than the woman, wearing a tee shirt and briefs, yawning and scratching himself on the belly. It looked like he was her cousin who had slept in the stuffy room but now had to go for a walk in order to free the bed.

The tourist stared at the bed. It was sagging and in the centre of the bed, rolled into a ball, was the dirtiest blanket he had ever seen. The woman (under the light of the single bulb in the room, she looked downright fat) saw him looking, picked up the blanket and put it in the corner of the room, replacing it with a yellowish bed sheet. Then she asked him what he wanted to do, using gestures when he did not understand a particular word. He wanted to do something that involved as little touching anything in this room, including her, as possible. Again, he asked how much but the woman told him not to worry about it. Then she helped him undress, put a condom on him and energetically took him in his mouth. The tourist, dazed, watched her curly head bob up and down in the cracked mirror on the wall next to the bed. After a while, the woman was convinced that he was not coming, sighed and took off her clothes and started to ride him. She had enormous black breasts which kept swaying about and hitting him in the face. The tourist kissed one of them, unconvincingly. The woman kept rocking on top of him with strong, sudden movements, until he finally came. When she stood up, some blood dripped down from her. She swiftly wiped it off with a paper napkin that she also used to wrap the bloodied condom in, looked around, did not see a trash bin and put the napkin in her purse.

The tourist dressed and asked what was going on. The woman explained that there was nothing to worry about, he was just too big. The tourist did not think that was the case but he did not know enough Spanish to argue. For the third time, he asked how much and the woman told him a sum in U.S. dollars that seemed too large. Besides, he did not have U.S. dollars or Cuban pesos because he had walked out on the seaside boulevard as soon as he arrived in the hotel, and he had not seen a single bank or exchange office. The woman listened to his explanation closely and repeated the same sum in euro. The tourist hesitated and she asked him if he was not pleased with her. He did not have an answer for this. The woman explained that the money was not just for her but also for her cousin that he had seen earlier and also her mother who did not live in Havana and had cancer. The tourist paid her.

The woman walked him back to the alley where she had caught him. The cousin was waiting patiently at the corner, leaning against the wall, so that he could go back to the room and sleep.

The tourist returned to his hotel, went up to his room with the ancient elevator which was crawling more slowly than he would have been able to climb the stairs, if only he knew where the stairs were, and had several glasses of rum one after the other. There was no television set in the room and his window looked on the opposite wall, so after a while he took the elevator back down to the patio of the hotel where a small band was playing, and had a couple of beers. On the walls of the corridors and the foyer were old sepia-coloured photographs of well-dressed men with moustaches. The labels next to the photographs identified them as legendary hit men and mob bosses, some of whom had kept rooms in this hotel all year round to run their business from.

The tourist went up to his room, switched on his laptop and wrote a review for the hotel in which he described it as a large house of spirits with dozens of rooms, each one keeping the memory of a dark betrayal or a bloody retribution. He was quite drunk and kept hitting the wrong keys on the keyboard, plus he had to leave his room several times with his notebook to squint at the photographs in the corridors and write down dates and names, paying no attention to the other hotel guests who walked by, but in the end he managed to finish his review a little past midnight. Of course, there was no wireless internet connection in the hotel, so the tourist saved the text file to send to the tourist website from the next place. Then he poured himself another rum but was not able to finish it because he fell asleep.

On the next morning, he felt sick on the bus to Varadero. When they stopped to use the restroom and take photographs at a road diner with a view to a very high bridge over the jungle, he shuffled off the bus and went to buy himself a beer.

He was not especially surprised to see the young couple – they were standing next to a souvenir stand, the young woman was trying on some plastic sunglasses and the young man was holding a mirror to her face so that she could see if they fit her. Dazed by the sun and the beer, the tourist did not know what to do or say, so he turned back and boarded the bus again, even though they had ten more minutes before they were to continue. The two of them did not notice him but he kept looking at them while they photographed themselves on the viewing platform in front of the bridge and pointed some things out to each other. The man was more restrained but he, too, seemed happy. The tourist shrugged, finished his beer and tried to sleep.

The hotel in Varadero had a very long and bombastic name which unsuccessfully tried to conceal the fact that it looked just like any other hotel on the coastline. The next morning, the tourist woke up and conscientiously tried out everything that was offered to the guests of the hotel, keeping notes.

Wearing trainers and gloves, he went down to the fitness-centre and worked out for forty-five minutes: ten minutes of running on the treadmill, ten minutes of rowing on the rowing machine, three sets of ten repetitions on a machine which imitated a bench press, three sets of ten repetitions on another machine which imitated a squat, three sets of ten repetitions on a third machine which imitated a pulley, and a total of one hundred repetitions on a fourth machine working out the abdominal muscles, divided in five sets of twenty repetitions each.

Wearing a tee shirt, bathing trunks and his new flip-flops, he went down to the spa and read the complete menu of procedures. He poured himself a plastic cup of water next to the machine in the corner and walked out of the spa, pretending to talk on the phone, motioning to the receptionist that he will be back in a minute.

Wearing the same outfit, he went down to the round pool in front of the hotel, left his tee shirt and his key card on a lounging chair, carefully put on swimming goggles and swam forty lengths down the diameter of the pool.

Then he went to the beach in front of the hotel, chose a lounging chair at the far end, equidistant to the sea and the bar, spread his towel, covered his body with an even layer of sunscreen and worked on his tan from four until six thirty. Meanwhile he finished a paperback and had three cocktails, brought to him on the lounging chair every forty-five minutes or so.

Wearing navy blue slacks, a light blue shirt, loafers and black socks, he went down to the hotel restaurant for dinner. He was the only person in the restaurant wearing socks.

The staff treated him with the peculiar kind condolence reserved for single guests in such hotels that he had gotten used to. If someone asked, he had a whole range of explanations at his disposal – everyday (his wife was held up by work at the bank but she would join him later), dramatic (they had been planning this trip for several months but a week before they were to go, he had come home early and caught her in bed with his best friend), macabre (he was certain that she would have enjoyed it here but he wanted to hope that she was in a good place, too).

No one ever asked.

The tourist had his second bottle of wine brought up to his room and sat on the balcony with his laptop on his knees to write the review for the hotel. He was looking at the other guests through a double screen: the plexiglass of the balcony wall and the French windows of the restaurant. They were opening their mouths and laughing but he could not hear anything. He wrote a review in which he described his day minute by minute. Then he scrolled up to the beginning of the text and carefully weeded out all the words which betrayed his real emotions. He sent it to the tourist website together with his review for the previous hotel in Havana.

On the next afternoon, the tourist was sitting on the balcony and drinking rum with crushed ice – this required frequent trips to the next bungalow as the ice machine in his own was out of order. He had finished a bottle of white wine at lunch, he had put up his feet on the parapet of the balcony and he was not sure that he would be able to walk properly when he had to go and fetch more ice. A hummingbird was flying around the bushes with long, wet leaves that grew in front of his balcony.

The young man appeared on the alley between the bungalows, wearing a towel on his shoulders. For the first time, he was not accompanied by the young woman. The tourist looked at him for a while, then he sighed, left his glass and stood up.

He found him on a lounging chair next to the pool. The young man offered him the next seat and the tourist eased himself down on the lounging chair. His temples were throbbing from the sun and the alcohol.

The two of them sat in silence for a while. Then the man asked the tourist if he was the one that he thought he was.

The tourist nodded.

The man explained that it was probably best to do it today as the young woman had gone on a trip to a dolphin-centre organised by the hotel and she would not be back until the early afternoon on the next day. His voice was calm, with no trace of excitement or worry. Then he asked the tourist if he had something particular in mind.

The tourist nodded again.

Then he cleared his throat, asked the man about his room number and told him to wait there in fifteen minutes. He stood up, went back to his own room and took out of his bag the small, very sharp kitchen knife that he had bought in Havana. The ice in the bucket that he had left next to the bottle of rum on the balcony had melted. The hummingbird was gone. He poured the water out in the bushes, put the knife in the bucket and closed the lid.

When the man opened the door for him, the tourist explained that the ice machine in his bungalow was out of order. The man nodded and let him in. There were no people on the alleys anyway, but the tourist was always careful about details. The man asked him if he wanted something to drink. The two of them sat facing each other – the tourist was sitting in an armchair and the man was sitting on the bed. The bed had been made by the maid and one of the towels was folded so that it looked like a swan. She did this every day when she came to clean the room, around eleven.

The two of them sipped from their glasses. The young man had rum, neat. He was still in his bathing trunks. He had a thin but wiry body with faded tattoos. He looked healthy. His eyes kept darting between the tourist and various objects in the room: the sandals of the young woman left on the floor, a wrinkled cotton jacket in the open wardrobe, the television set left on with the sound off.

The tourist asked him if he was sure. The man replied that he was completely sure. Sometimes the tourist asked them about the reason but the young man was acting so business-like that the question seemed inappropriate.

The client sat on the bed and drank rum while the tourist stood up, walked into the bathroom and filled the tub with hot water. While he was inside, he took out the knife from the ice bucket, wiped off his own fingerprints and left it on the edge of the bathtub. Then he returned to the room and explained to the man how to cut his wrists – down, not across. The man listened to him, nodded a couple of times, swallowed and poured the rest of his rum down his throat. The tourist softly asked him if he preferred that the tourist perform this. The client shook his head. The tourist told him that he will stay in the room but in a few minutes he will go to check on him and help him if he needed help. The man nodded some more, then he took in a breath, stood up and went to the bathroom.

The tourist reached for the remote and turned on the sound of the television.

In a few minutes, he went to the bathroom. The man had done a perfect job. He was lying on his back, with his head resting on the edge of the tub, his eyes closed. The warm water was red.

The tourist put his glass in the ice bucket and used a towel to wipe down the remote and the doorknobs. Then he went out of the client's room, returned to his own room and sat on the balcony. If the young woman did not come back early from her organised trip to the dolphin centre, the man was going to be found by the maid on the next morning.

The tourist opened his laptop and connected to the other website that he was working for. He found the young man's profile and changed the status of the order from "accepted" to "completed". The rest of the pay would be transferred automatically. The money passed through several offshore accounts, following a scheme that the tourist had never attempted to comprehend, just like the security system of the website itself – everything worked flawlessly and there had never been any mistakes.

The clients were people who had their reasons to want to end their lives, but also had their reasons not to do it themselves, or were not able to. Sometimes, as with the young man in the bathtub, they were actually able to do it themselves, but they needed a little support. After passing through several levels of selection to prove that their intentions were serious, the clients registered in the waiting list with their location. The tourist (and the others like him – he assumed that there were others like him, but he did not know any of them) chose and accepted the order and the client was informed about the approximate completion date.

The tourist always tried to make it look like a suicide or an accident. Most often, the clients cooperated by leaving suicide notes, travelling alone and avoiding crowded places. Sometimes they even managed to commit suicide before he was able to organise the completion of the order. (The tourist suspected that some people preferred to end their own lives but ordered an assisted suicide as a backup.)

Nevertheless, he took precautions: he never completed more than one order in the same place or in the same way, he never used instruments more than once and he avoided talking to other people except the staff of hotels and airlines, with which he tried to leave no impression at all.

Besides, he had the perfect alibi: a published and dated hotel review from every place that he had ever been to.

The young woman returned on the next day. The tourist, as well as the other guests of the hotel, saw next to nothing of the summary police investigation: the hotel administration was extremely motivated to make everything happen as discreetly as possible, so that nobody would cut their holiday short.

The tourist stayed for as long as he had planned, swimming, eating and reading in regular hours. He did not make any acquaintances. Nobody wanted to make his.

A few days later, the hotel minivan left him at Havana airport – probably the last airport in the world where smoking was still not banned – and the tourist disappeared in the crowd.

PART ONE

4. Dublin

The tourist loathed corporate events. Corporate events were the turf of people from all over the world who either knew each other professionally or could not wait to meet in person, and he was in neither of those two categories. Moreover, corporations seemed to value affability, and manifestations of affability invariably caused him to feel threatened. To top it all, the corporate event was held in Dublin, organised by the local branch of a Japanese manufacturer of home electronics, and the Irish themselves were affable by nature, so that the manifestations of affability were a lot more frequent and intensive.

The Japanese manufacturer of home electronics was one of the principal advertisers in the new film from the series that chronicled the adventures of a world-famous secret agent. In the film, the secret agent – played by a world-famous British actor – used a camera from the most recent product line of the manufacturer to photograph some shady characters and upload the photographs directly to the headquarters of British intelligence. The idea of the corporate event was for a large number of journalists from all over the world to attend a large number of opening nights for the new film about the secret agent, held in elite cinemas in various world capitals. The journalists were equipped with cameras which were the same model as the one featured in the film, using some kind of revolutionary hypersensitive technology which allowed them to take photographs in very low light conditions without a flash. Every journalist was supposed to take a large number of photographs during the opening night which they could upload immediately to the specially designed website of the manufacturer, as the cameras had a wireless connection to the internet as well. The advertising agency of the Japanese manufacturer was going to use the very large number of photographs taken in this manner to compile the television commercial for the new camera.

The only reason for the tourist to pose as an accredited journalist at this corporate event was that his new client was a regional manager for the corporation. The biggest problem was that the client did not behave like a man who wanted to commit suicide at all.

The regional manager was a fifty-year-old Irishman in rude health. He had a pink face, white hair and a jovial smile. He was portly, but not overly so, and as the tourist was able to see for himself during the business breakfast in the press-centre of the corporate event, he had an excellent appetite and a sense of humour which – combined with his high position in the corporation – made the guests on his table shake with laughter.

After breakfast, the journalists were given some free time to explore the city. Most of them plunged into the historical quarter by the river. The tourist crossed the river in the opposite direction. There were not so many pubs and historical sights here and most of the people on the streets were locals who were not paying attention to him. The tourist did not like tourists. They paid attention to everything.

There was a modern monument in the middle of a square – a shining steel column which was rose high above the adjacent buildings and looked as if it was needle-sharp at the top. The tourist sat on a bench at the edge of the square and looked at the needle for a while. The needle seemed to glow, outlined against the gray sky.

For lunch, the journalists were driven by bus from the press centre to the restaurant of an expensive hotel in the suburbs where they would have the chance to meet in person the star of the film about the secret agent. The meeting was arranged like this: the journalists were seated in groups of about ten people each in the restaurant and served light lunch; after a while, the actor arrived in the restaurant as well, causing mild excitement; and he started working the tables, pausing next to each one, talking and joking with the journalists at the table before he moved to the next one.

The actor was one of the most affable people the tourist had ever seen. He was taller than he looked on the screen, he was tanned, and he had thick hair and shining teeth. His suit was immaculate. Clearly, he had no trouble conversing with hundreds of strangers, seated in groups of about ten people each, most of whom did not even speak English as a first language – he always found something to talk about, he often laughed and all the time he looked like he was having a great time.

The tourist started sweating even before the actor had reached his table. When he arrived, he shook everyone's hand with his big, warm, strong hand. Then he turned to the tourist and asked him a question. The tourist did not know what to say in response. A young woman with large breasts answered the question for him – she was seated next to the tourist and introduced herself as an editor in the Russian edition of a world-famous men's magazine. The actor listened to her very carefully, then his face suddenly brightened and he said something that made everyone on the table laugh. Then he thanked them for their time and moved on to the next table.

The tourist bent over his plate. The Russian journalist caught his eye and smiled encouragingly. He nodded to her and ate a cauliflower.

After lunch, he returned to his hotel on the river, opposite the old quarter. There was a full tea set in his room and he made some strong black tea for himself before he opened his laptop and wrote a review for the hotel which was based on the fact that the hotel was located opposite and not in the old quarter, with all the positive consequences of this. (There was no pub on the ground floor which had been opened back in the seventeenth century which meant that there was no possibility of being woken up by drunk singing at three thirty in the morning, either; the building was not a historical monument which meant that the floor plans met modern standards instead of those preceding the invention of the elevator, when the first floor had been the most prestigious one, etc.)

Afterwards, he studied the regional manager's order again. Attached to it was the complete programme for the corporate event which was to go on and on with a series of opening nights for the film all over the world. The tourist had been given an accreditation for each one. He was sincerely hoping that he would not have to attend them all. The sooner he managed to complete the order, the better. Besides, he still did not understand why this successful man who clearly loved his job wanted to kill himself. Perhaps he knew something that ordinary people did not. Perhaps his corporation was threatened by some crisis which was going to wreak havoc on its financial results. Perhaps he had a big life insurance policy and he wanted to leave enough money for his family before he went bankrupt.

The tourist shrugged and closed his laptop.

The corporate event continued with an evening screening of the film which took place in a huge, bustling night club downtown. The club had three floors which looked like they had been designed by different, fiercely competitive interior designers. There were wrought-iron balustrades, grand pianos and potted tropical plants. There were suspended ceilings, floor lights and stained glass. There was a cinema-sized screen for the film but not enough places to sit and the tourist retreated to the back of the top floor where he thought it was least probable that someone would take his photograph by mistake with their brand new company-provided camera.

The screening was a great success. Before the film started, the lead actor himself stood up before the screen, behaving just as affably as he had during the lunch with the journalists. The rude joke that he told caused such excitement with the Irish organisers of the event that they applauded him for several minutes. Some of the journalists had not managed to turn off the flash on their cutting-edge cameras and they started going off everywhere in the club, so several more minutes passed before the company representatives had found the guilty journalists and assisted them. Then the film finally started.

The tourist did not watch the film. He was watching the client. The regional manager was seated at a table on the first floor, near the screen, with several other men in suits and ties. He seemed to be having a blast. There was a bottle of champagne on the table but the manager was drinking beer. After the fourth pint, he said something to the others that made them laugh, stood up and disappeared in the back of the hall. The tourist walked down the stairs from the third floor, found the restrooms and went inside. The manager was there, facing a urinal, with his back to him. When he heard the door, he turned his head and gave the tourist a friendly greeting. He returned the greeting, then he entered one of the booths. His pulse was racing. Before he could do something, several other men walked into the restroom, talking among themselves. One of them stood next to the manager's urinal and made a joke. The manager laughed loudly.

The tourist stayed in the booth until everyone had left.

Then he returned to his spot in the back of the third floor, stopped a passing waiter and ordered a double whiskey. The film had reached the decisive third act and the secret agent was trying to destroy the secret base of the sinister organisation, causing lots of loud noises. The tourist finished his whiskey and ordered another.

After the film ended, he was approached by a young woman with large breasts. She was wearing the same tight-fitting knitted dress that she had been wearing for the lunch with the British actor; otherwise the tourist would not have recognised her. The woman offered her hand and introduced herself. The tourist hesitated before he introduced himself in turn. The woman explained to him that several of the local representatives of the corporation had invited her and her female colleagues from leading Russian magazines to join them in some other club. She clearly had a hard time talking in English and the tourist tried to answer in Russian but she did not understand what he was saying. He switched back to the featureless international English that he used most often to communicate with people all over the world, and repeated that this was great. The young woman nodded impatiently and again offered him her hand. The tourist left his glass and took it.

The local representatives of the corporation were young men with ruddy faces and loosened ties who looked slightly bewildered when she returned with him to their table. The tourist felt bewildered as well and was ready to leave anytime, but the Russian girl kept holding on to his hand or his elbow. The young men concentrated once more on her friends, most of whom were dazzling.

The other club was nearby but it was completely different – it was in a private apartment on the top floor of a quiet building, with heavy furniture and understated paintings on the walls. There was a bar in the kitchen, tended by an older man in a white shirt and a black bowtie. The tourist had a few more drinks. The Russian girl had a few glasses of wine. The conversation was not running smoothly, perhaps because of the language barrier. At some point in the evening, she stepped closer to him, looked up, stood on her toes and kissed him on the mouth.

Much later, the two of them went to his hotel. The Russian journalist was experiencing some kind of late-night rush and pulled back playfully when the tourist tried to make her lie on the bed. For some reason, now she did not want to kiss. She insisted that they must drink more. He turned towards the minibar to check what was left in it, but then she hugged him from behind, pulling him back to the bed. He tried to kiss her, but she started laughing and twisting under him and insisting that they must drink more.

Finally, they had sex in several different positions. The tourist came and kept moving back and forth for a while, unsure if she had come as well, but the girl slid off him, rolled over onto her back and declared that they must drink more.

After they had emptied the minibar, she left. When the tourist woke up in the morning, he found her business card on the desk in his room. For the next few days, he used the card to mark the page in the paperback novel that he was reading, but then he abandoned it, together with the finished book, in a room in a hotel in Brazil.

5. London – Paris – Sao Paolo

The tourist was afraid of flying, even though he had been on more than fifty flights since the start of this year alone. Before every one of those flights, he had not been able to sleep properly, and after every one of them, he had had stomach problems, heart palpitations and (in the case of longer flights), jetlag-induced stupor which was stronger when he had flown east but equally unpleasant in both directions.

Most of all, he was afraid of taking off – after the plane reached cruising altitude, he felt somewhat calmer and was even able to eat or sleep, as long as there was no sudden turbulence (sudden turbulence horrified him); and he was irrationally placid during landing, although statistically, landing was just as dangerous as taking off. But taking off was a terror. During every take-off, the tourist slowly counted to a hundred and eighty, usually with his eyes closed, as he had read somewhere that most crashes occurred during the first three minutes after the plane left the runway. When he reached a hundred and eighty, he opened his eyes and cautiously looked out the window (over his neighbour or neighbours, as he reserved aisle seats whenever he could). Some planes had the nasty tendency to bank sharply precisely at this moment, immediately sending him into another counting session with his eyes closed.

And if there was something that he hated even more than taking off, it was connecting flights – because he had to take off just a couple of hours after he had landed.

During the next two days, he was going to be on a total of four flights and the last three of them were connected.

The tourist arrived in London on a low-cost flight which deposited him – an hour and thirty minutes late – at a small airport outside the city. The airport looked like a bus station crossed with a supermarket. He walked around it until he found the stop for the minibuses to London and spent the next two hours in roundabouts and ridiculous traffic jams all the way to one of the main train stations in the city where the route of the minibus ended. He had reserved a room in a featureless small hotel near the station, but he was not prepared for how featureless and small the hotel would actually be – it was in a long row of identical houses behind the station, all of them hotels similar to his, and his room was so small that the only window was the size of a plane window, situated at pavement level, with a view to a steel bicycle rack.

He was so late that he did not have time to shower, so he left his bag in the room and took the subway to the south bank of the river where the next screening of the film about the secret agent was going to take place.

This time, the film was to be shown in an open-air theatre built especially for the purpose on a riverside square. The screen was put up on the wall of a building which the organisers proudly explained was actually a film museum. The day was long and they had to wait for dark to show the film, so there were lots of drinks and affable conversations. The tourist ate some finger food and retreated to the back of the square with two glasses of white wine. When he finished them, he went to the bar and ordered two more glasses of white wine, as if he was with someone.

But he was not with anyone. With a few exceptions, the accredited journalists were not the same as in Dublin, the editor from the Russian men's magazine had gone back to

Moscow and, most importantly, there was no sign of his client.

The tourist waited until the film started to make absolutely sure but the cheerful man with the pink face and the white hair never showed up. This was ghastly as it meant that he had to go on to the next stop of the programme of the corporate event to meet him again.

According to the programme, the next screening of the film was going to take place on a small island at the base of the Iguazu Falls on the border of Argentine and Brazil.

He left before the film ended and walked back to the hotel, passing throngs of tourists and noisy crowds of Londoners who had had a few drinks. He had to get up very early on the following morning to catch the minibus which would take him back to the airport outside the city and he wanted to go to sleep immediately.

But he did not. The air in his room was so stuffy that he had to leave the pavement window open, but there was a continuous stream of people outside, talking in loud voices, kicking things along the pavement, shouting and – in a particularly unpleasant case – singing a football anthem. The tourist went to sleep very late in the night and it seemed that he was woken immediately – by some kind of terrifying noise. He looked at his watch. It was four in the morning. Gray light was oozing in from the window. The terrifying noise was caused by a street cleaning truck passing outside. The tourist tried to go back to sleep but the street cleaning truck was followed by a number of other trucks loading the shops, stopping at the streetlight on the corner and roaring off again. A little later, the first motorcycles of the day joined them. The tourist sighed, rolled over on his back and stared at the ceiling.

He felt tired and irritable when he walked to the stop for the minibuses going to the airport. The traffic jams in the morning were even more unbearable than those on the previous evening. The tourist sat with his forehead pressed to the glass of the window, sluggishly following with his eyes the cars in the neighbouring lane which were always going faster than the ones in his.

He managed to go to sleep on the plane to Paris, but the flight attendant woke him up to ask him if he wanted tea or coffee. Before he could sleep again, the plane began the descent towards the airport and the loudspeakers directly above his head crackled to life, broadcasting meaningless notifications about putting on seatbelts, putting up seats and tables, turning off all electronic devices, local time, Paris weather, thank you for flying with us and we hope to see you again very soon, more information about the airline flights on the internet, the numbers of gates for connecting flights and thank you once more for your attention. The tourist apathetically wondered who was speaking and whether or not they were going to crash during the landing because the pilot had been too busy listening to the sound of his own voice to fly the plane.

The airport in Paris was a logistical nightmare. It took the tourist just several minutes to reach the terminal for his connecting flight but then he had to spend several hours in line with families with a number of small children who were throwing tantrums simultaneously, and Greek couples who were talking on their mobile phones incessantly and so loudly that they probably did not need mobile phones to be heard where they were calling. The woman in front wore such a lot of jewellery that she had to go back four times before they let her through. The tourist passed on the first try but it was already too late – his flight was supposed to have taken off twenty minutes ago. He ran all the way to the gate where he found out that his flight to Sao Paolo was two hours late.

There was not a single available seat at the gate. Most seats were occupied by passengers who had clearly been there a very long time, sleeping with their shoes off or looking around with the heavy, unfocused gaze of people who have already taken a good look at everything there is to see around, several times.

The tourist had a large strong coffee and used the toilet twice. He was starting to feel some kind of weight behind his eyelids that he was only able to alleviate by closing his eyes. At last, he sat down on the floor next to the wall and rested his forehead against his knees.

They announced that the flight was going to be an additional forty minutes late before they finally allowed them to board the plane.

After they took off, ate their dinner, opened the plastic bags containing their blankets, sleeping masks and the earphones for the small screens on the backs of the seat in front, the woman sitting next to the tourist expressed a wish to use the toilet. The only way for her to reach the toilet involved the tourist getting up from his own seat to make way for her and then standing in the aisle until she came back.

When most of the passengers settled in for the night, sleeping or staring at the screens in front, the tourist was suddenly jolted awake by some kind of inexplicable energy. He could not even imagine going to sleep despite the soft lights and the reassuring white noise from the engines of the plane, transporting him over the ocean. He calculated the time in London – the last place where he had had a semblance of a night's sleep – but the result contained no meaningful information whatsoever. Cautiously, trying not to wake the woman in the next seat, he reached up and switched on the spotlight above his head. Then he read the international newspaper that he had taken from the rack at the entrance of the plane from the first page to the last, completed the crossword and the jumbled-letters game. Then he switched on the display in front and watched several episodes of a show about criminal investigators and the first half of a film about a man who was paralysed by a rare disease and was only able to move one of his eyelids before he gave up and stared at the map which showed the plane crossing the Atlantic with the changing numbers of the covered distance and the distance remaining to be covered. Finally, he began to relax again, turned off the screen and rested his head back to go to sleep.

At this moment, the woman sitting next to him woke up, shifted in her seat and softly nudged him because she wanted to go to the toilet.

When they landed in Sao Paolo, the tourist was not surprised in the least that he had missed his connecting flight to Cataratas del Iguazu, the small airport near the waterfalls. The next flight of the airline for which he had a pre-paid ticket by the organisers of the corporate event left in ten hours. The tourist decided that he preferred to spend ten hours at the airport instead of going to Sao Paolo. He felt more at home in featureless, international places where everything was simultaneously unfamiliar and the same as everywhere else.

He sat in a café and had a croissant and a lethally strong double espresso. He was so exhausted already that his facial muscles tended to slack off and he had to be careful not to sit with his mouth hanging open. He devised a plan how to kill the time until his flight. The plan consisted of one-hour modules (reading a magazine, lunch, watching television in one of the airport bars), separated by ten-minute walks which should help him to wake up a little.

Several hours later, he found himself in a faux-English pub where he drank down four pints and watched a full football game. The team he had chosen for their colours lost.

Several more hours later he had rested his forehead on a window looking on a runway. He saw a large bird which flew down and landed on the wing of a parked plane. There was another, smaller bird which kept flying in circles around it, dashing towards the larger bird as if it wanted to attack it but always pulling back at the last moment. Oblivious, the larger bird stretched its neck upwards, tossed up something that it had been carrying in its beak, caught it and swallowed it whole, flapping its wings once. The smaller bird circled around it a few more times disconsolately, then it flew up and away.

Several hours after that, the gate for his flight was opened. The tourist did not remember how he had gotten on the plane.

The plane took off. He closed his eyes and started counting to a hundred and eighty. He made it to eighteen before he fell asleep.

6. Puerto Iguazu

The tourist did not feel comfortable when he was wet. He had no problem with showers and baths, but uncontrolled water – in the form of rain, humidity, rivers, seas and oceans – violated his personal comfort.

When he got off the plane at the airport of Cataratas del Iguazu, the hot wet night met him like a slap. The airport was so small that it had no jet bridges or even buses to transport passengers from the aircraft to the arrivals hall. The plane landed on the strip, taxied to the single-floor building and when they disembarked, there was a man outside who showed them where to go without saying a word. The air smelled of the jungle.

It was one thirty in the morning and there were only two or three people waiting in the arrivals hall which was the same room as the departures hall. One of them was holding a sign with the name under which the tourist was accredited as a journalist for the corporate event. The tourist approached him; the man shook his hand and took his only bag.

There was a minivan waiting outside. The two of them boarded the minivan and drove off. The cleared ground around the airport was soon replaced by dense forest, with the trees overhanging the road. The driver turned to the tourist and said something in Spanish from which the tourist gathered that the hotel was very nice and it was in the jungle. He thought that this was just an expression – something they told all arriving guests, like the seaside hotels that are always said to be on the beach – but in a few minutes the driver turned the wheel all the way to the left and the engine howled when the minivan climbed onto a steep gravel road that did indeed go straight into the jungle. The headlights revealed a tangle of lianas. The tourist thought that this could have been the setting of a perfect murder, but this time he was on the other side.

After a while, lights could be seen through the trees and the minivan went out of the jungle and onto the alley in front of the hotel's main building. The hotel was very nice indeed. The villas were connected with hanging wooden bridges and the abstract-shaped pool glowed with a soft pale green light. Raccoons crawled in the grass among the buildings. The tourist got off the minivan and listened – he could hear birds and a constant, mighty humming. The driver smiled and explained that it came from the waterfalls.

The tourist checked in, went to his room, unpacked his luggage, took a hot shower and sighed when he finally lay down on the bed.

Thirty minutes later, the phone in his room exploded with a deafening ringing sound.

He jumped up – his heart was beating wildly and for a few seconds he could not remember where he was – and picked up the receiver. They were calling from reception to notify him that the programme of the corporate event required the presence of all accredited journalists in the hotel lobby in thirty minutes.

There about twenty blinking men and women in the hotel lobby. The unduly cheerful organisers gave them each a black waterproof with the logo of the Japanese electronics corporation. The regional manager who was the tourist's client was not there.

They boarded two minivans and started off through the jungle again. The guide explained that they were going to drive them to the viewing platforms above the waterfalls before the sun rose, so that they could see them (and take photographs) in the pre-dawn light. There was awe in the guide's voice when he told them that in his thirty years as a guide, not once had he brought a group to the waterfalls during the night, as the whole region was a nature reserve and the rules forbade the entrance of tourists after sunset so that they would not bother the animals who hunted and fed in the dark.

When they got off the minivans, the noise of the waterfalls was much stronger. They gave them each a flashlight, then they took off through the jungle along a path covered with perforated sheet metal. The air was so humid that heavy drops were crawling down the leaves above their heads. The tourist put on the waterproof and put up the hood, but several drops still managed to find a way down his back. It was surprisingly cold.

When they reached the platforms with the view to the monstrous whitish shapes of the waterfalls, the morning dew was suddenly out. It felt like someone had thrown a bucket of cold water in his face. The moisture came right out of the air. In a few seconds, all his clothes were already clinging to him, despite the waterproof. When he looked at his hands, his fingers were puffy, as if he had spent too much time in the bath. The special camera that he had been equipped with was still smugly operational but the tourist had no desire to take photographs. He stood in the corner of the viewing platform; his hands stuck under his waterproof, and tried not to let his teeth chatter.

His client did not come to the breakfast in the hotel restaurant, either.

Later in the day, it transpired that the island that the corporate event guests were supposed to be standing on to watch the film about the secret agent projected straight onto the face of the waterfalls was currently two metres underwater. While the organisers were looking for a new setting for the screening, the journalists were offered a boat ride at the base of the waterfalls. The regional manager from Ireland finally appeared and the tourist boarded the minivan that he was riding on, but when they reached the pier with the boats, the manager said he was going to wait for them in the minivan. The tourist boarded the first boat, clenching his teeth.

The afternoon programme included a visit to a butterfly reserve in the vicinity, but the tourist missed the departure time on purpose and stayed in his room. After the journalists left the hotel, he went down to the reception area and called for a taxi. During the drive through the jungle, he asked the driver about the place that he needed. The driver was not surprised – after all, they were in South America where the usage of exotic plants for medicinal purposes had a long and respected tradition. The tourist asked him to wait in front of the little shop, found what he was looking for, paid in cash, went back to the car and told the driver to take him back to the hotel.

In the evening, it started to rain. Dressed in their identical waterproofs, the accredited journalists and the organisers of the event gathered in the hotel lobby. There were a few trucks waiting outside, modified for carrying passengers. An energetic young man who had the guest list asked the journalists to board the trucks but the tourist noticed the regional manager climbing into a jeep parked a little further.

The trucks crawled on a dirt road through the jungle for almost an hour, sinking in the mud. Finally, they reached a clearing with a few miserable ruins at the edge. In some of them, there were burning fires and glimmering television sets. Someone explained that they were in a loggers' settlement, using the word "authentic". The tourist thought that a more precise term would have been "appalling".

At the end of the clearing, where the jungle began, there was a screen. The journalists huddled close to each other, as if their proximity could protect them from the rain. The raindrops drummed on their plastic waterproofs. There was a marquee put up next to the parked trucks, with an improvised bar that served hot drinks and alcohol. The tourist retreated under it.

Fifteen minutes later, the regional manager appeared out of the gloom outside, shaking the mud off his shoes. When he reached the marquee, he took off his hood and grunted, sounding amused. His eyes met the tourist's and the manager nodded in a friendly manner. His eyes were bright and full of cheer, as usual. The tourist tried to smile back but did not succeed and quickly raised his glass to his mouth to conceal his grimace. The manager walked to the bar, made a few jokes to the bartenders and procured a few glasses. Then he put up his hood, took the glasses and went back out into the rain, among the crowd, where the only light came from the flickering reflection on the screen.

The tourist followed him.

He was holding the largest needle from the hotel sewing kit, dipped in the plant poison extract that he had bought from the herbal shop in the small town. Back in his room, he had read a few articles about the plant – the symptoms were those of food poisoning, followed by a heart attack. Seizure was not guaranteed, but on the other hand, most traces of the poison decomposed in a few hours. The tourist decided to take that risk – or rather, he decided that the manager was going to take that risk. After all, they were in the jungle. There must have been insects here whose bite was more deadly than the needle in his hand.

He followed the manager through the crowd, waited for the right moment to walk past him when the client's attention was completely focused on the glasses in his hands, and stuck him in the right gluteus. Then he kept walking through the crowd until he reached the end of the clearing, dropped the needle in the deep mud and stepped on it. Finally, he returned under the marquee, took another glass and patiently prepared to see the rest of the film about the secret agent – for the last time, he hoped.

When they returned to the hotel, two of the organisers were waiting for them in front of the entrance, armed with large black trash bags. After they had waded through the mud for a few hours, cleaning their shoes seemed impossible. They were told that they could leave them in the bags and the organisers would take care that their shoes went to people who needed them. In any case, it was not advisable to walk back inside the hotel wearing them. On the other side of the entrance, two hotel employees had set out a large number of hotel slippers.

The tourist sat down on the steps to take off his shoes. In the light coming from the hotel lobby, the mud was bright red. After he took them off, his hands were also covered in red mud. He had only one other pair of shoes but he had no choice so he dropped them in the charity trash bag and went inside.

He went up to his room, took a hot shower, dried himself, dressed in his dry clothes, put on his other pair of shoes and went down to dinner. This had been the last screening in the programme of the corporate event, so there was a full hour of exchanging business cards, looking at thousands of photographs (despite the legendary technical characteristics of the new cameras, almost nothing could be discerned on them), humorous thank-you speeches from the organisers and some of the journalists, apologies for the change in the programme and the weather conditions in the Iguazu waterfalls region and South America in general, and promises that the next corporate event was going to be even bigger than this one. Fortunately, there was a bar in the hotel lobby which supplied the tourist with a regular flow of excellent Argentinian red.

The regional manager did not make an appearance which must have been such a drastic breach of corporate ethics that one of the representatives of the company felt the need to explain his absence to the journalists. He had stayed in his room, she said, because he did not feel so good. Nothing serious, probably just a case of food poisoning.

Then they were seated at large round tables, decorated with table name tags, and the efficient silent waiters served the first course. The tourist ordered a bottle of the same red that they were serving at the bar and poured both for himself and the woman who was seated on his left. The name on her tag looked Romanian and he tried a few phrases in French before they switched to the customary international English.

The tourist swirled the wine in his glass and leaned back in his chair. For the first time in a very long time, he was feeling dry. He intended to remain indoors until he left this continent. The Romanian woman smiled at him and handed him her bottle of mineral water because she could not open it herself.

The tourist smiled back, put his glass on the table and twisted the plastic cap. It turned out to be easier than he had expected.

In fact, it was so easy that half of the water from the bottle ended up in his lap.

7. Athens

The tourist felt nervous when he was using the subway – especially in unfamiliar places, and he was always in unfamiliar places. He preferred to walk whenever possible, and when it was not possible, he took a taxi – but the receptionist at his Athens hotel had told him that there was a subway station right outside the entrance and the next one on the line was right outside the new museum; and after his experience in the taxi from the airport, the tourist was determined to avoid taxis until he was safely out of Greece.

Which is why he was riding a horribly overcrowded subway train right now, trying not to touch anyone, while the people all around him were pushing him, stepping on his feet, breathing down his neck and talking on their mobile phones right next to his ear.

The night before, he arrived late and took a taxi from the stop in front of the airport terminal for arriving passengers. He expected traffic jams, but Athens surprised him with a system of highways, with huge brightly lit shopping malls flying by. The average speed of the taxi was a hundred kilometres per hour – even when they passed through tolling points, the driver hardly lifted his foot off the gas pedal – but even so, they had been travelling on the highway for about forty minutes when the tourist asked what was going on. By this time, he was fairly certain that he had seen a particular brightly lit shopping mall fly by at least twice. The driver shrugged and embarked on a long explanation about the upcoming general elections and the rallies and protesting demonstrations which were blocking the whole city. The tourist patiently listened to the explanation as he had nothing else to do.

When they stopped in front of the hotel, he had to pay the accrued highway toll and some kind of extra tax for taking the taxi from the airport in addition to the already fabulous sum on the meter. The tourist had never paid so much for a taxi ride. He did not have the money in cash but the driver assured him that it was no problem to pay with a credit card. The tourist paid, without trying to argue or bring the price down. He always acted like this – even in countries where it was commonly accepted for the customer to try to bring the price down and the vendors were actually insulted when he did not. (Actually, he did not know for a fact whether Greece was not one of those countries.)

The hotel was repulsive. It faced the highway where cars and motorcycles kept screaming by in spite of the late hour. It was a "business hotel" – a high, narrow building with claustrophobically crammed rooms – with a striptease bar attached to it. The room of the tourist was small and foul and the howl of the cars on the highway filtered through the closed windows. The bathroom was one of the most cramped spaces he had ever seen. The small television set, mounted on a loose brace over the bed, was operated by an ancient remote wrapped in dirty plastic tape, and offered a selection of news and talk shows in Greek and no less than five different porn channels, two of which were currently showing anal sex. (In one case, with triple penetration.)

Before he went to the bathroom to try and brush his teeth without bruising his elbows against the walls on both sides, he checked his profile on the other website.

The client had left him a message.

The message said that the client was going to wait for him on the terrace of the new museum at eleven on the following day.

The tourist was relieved to get off the subway but it was not much better on the street. There were crowds everywhere – tourists, locals, street vendors, and police – which congested at street corners, waited to cross the street and talked in dozens of different languages. He was further troubled by the thought that he was probably standing in a spot where this had been going on for thousands of years. The tourist had seen the poster pillars in Belgrade which in a few years bulged out to several times their size by the layers of paper plastered on top of each other – like artificial trees with rings that marked days and weeks instead of years. Every once in a while, the city sent someone with a chainsaw to cut through to the base and peel off the paper so that they could start to use them again. Athens reminded him of those pillars – the same base that people were living on over and over, for millennia.

The new museum was opposite the ancient hill dotted with ruins and crawling lines of tourists with cameras, and it was a surprisingly sober building of glass. The tourist paid the symbolic entrance fee, entered and went up on the second floor where there was a terrace with a café. All the seats outside were taken, so the tourist went to the end of the terrace and looked at the hill opposite.

The girl came to stand next to him. The tourist looked at her, hidden behind his sunglasses. She was as tall as he was, with long limbs and fingers, dressed in several layers of shapeless clothes in earth colours that would have been in fashion in the Athens from the time of the ruins on the hill. She wore beaded sandals. So she was really as tall as he was.

The girl told him to turn around and take his sunglasses off. The tourist hesitated, and then obeyed. Without a word, she nodded at the glass façade of the building which rose directly in front of them. It reflected the hill behind their backs. He looked more carefully and realised what he was looking at. The girl suddenly smiled.

The new museum was built in such a way that its façade reflected the actual hill which provided the artefacts exhibited in the museum. The girl enthusiastically explained (in accurate English tinged with a coarse unfamiliar accent that he did not even try to place) that the exhibits were situated on the various floors of the museum in such a way that the positions of the temples on the hill were reflected in the façade precisely on the level of the museum which hosted the findings from those temples.

Then the girl offered him her hand and shook his with her long, sinewy fingers. She was the client, of course.

They were silent for a while. On the opposite side of the square in front of the museum entrance, under the ancient hill, there was something like a moat that looked several thousand years old. While they were looking at it, a subway train clattered along the bottom of the moat. There were so many people crossing the small square that the tourist started to feel dizzy and moved to stand with his back to them, facing the girl. Then he asked her to tell him about herself.

She was happy to do it. She wanted to see the ancient wonders of the world and she had planned a detailed route through the Middle East, the Mediterranean and the Balkans that she had mostly completed. The tourist was not interested in ancient history and most of the places that she talked about with such enthusiasm did not mean anything to him. He asked her why she wanted to die.

Instead of answering the question, she asked him about his job. The tourist told her about the tourist website which published his hotel reviews. The natural impulse of the contributors who worked for it was to seek out the best, the most interesting and exotic hotels in the world and then to write amazing reviews about them, but in time he had found out that the users of the website usually looked for information on more mainstream, even featureless hotels, and they preferred to know the truth about them, so his job actually consisted of travelling alone all the time and describing what he saw. The girl pointed out that he had nothing to complain about; people chose their jobs and not the other way around.

The tourist did not know what to say to this.

Then the girl was suddenly all business, she took out a notebook and wrote down for him the name and the address of the youth hostel in Istanbul that she was planning to stay in on the next day. Before the tourist could object, she turned and walked away.

The tourist followed her with his eyes until she disappeared in the crowd. Of course, he could have followed her and found a way to end her life right then. It was almost what was expected of him – people who paid someone else to kill them because they were not able to commit suicide usually preferred an element of surprise to avoid the trauma of the conscious decision to put an end to their life at a specific point in time.

But he did not want to kill her.

In fact, he wanted to see her again.

8. Istanbul

The tourist did not mind waiting when he was expecting a particular event to happen at a previously announced hour – but he did mind surprises. He was a master of killing time when it was four hours at the airport, but when he did not know what he was waiting for, when and how something was going to happen and how important it would turn out to be, he felt painfully anxious.

He stood in the middle of something that the guides called "an underground water reservoir", but it looked more like a flooded throne room with hundreds of columns. There was a wooden walkway above the water to reach the opposite side of the hall. The huge head of a stone statue lay in the water next to the walkway, as if cut off from the body. The head lay on its side with a patient, almost kind expression, as it must have done for the last ten centuries. The tourist looked at it for a while, then he abruptly turned and walked back to the exit to return to his hotel.

He arrived on the previous morning and checked in a solid hotel from an international chain which he found in the waiting list of the tourist website. Then he took a taxi (there were tee-shirts saying "I survived a taxi ride in Istanbul" sold everywhere, but the experience proved far less dramatic) and went to the address the girl had given him. His hotel was on the Asian side of the city, with a view to the bridge and the straits. Her youth hostel was in the fashionable bohemian district on the European side, with a view to a narrow alley lined with bars and antique bookshops. The boy at the reception had a trendy mop of hair and rings on his eyebrows and his bottom lip; he checked in his computer and told him that the girl was actually going to arrive on the next day. She had called to modify her reservation after she had decided to visit Ephesus first.

The tourist thanked him, went back outside and took an aimless walk. It was foggy and drizzly. He walked into a bar and had two drinks. When he went back outside, the rain was stronger. He put up his collar and decided to return to his hotel.

He walked down to the water. The fashionable alleys with fashionable young people who looked the same as the young people in any other European city quickly gave way to a maze of bazaars, fish stalls and workshops, crowded exclusively by men with moustaches. The air was filled with the sharp smells of food, tobacco and waste. Oriental music burst out of the open doors of the workshops.

On the bridge which led to the Asian side stood a dozen fishermen with waterproofs, each of whom was manning a dozen fishing rods leaning on the railing. They had parked their cars next to the curb with their doors open so that they could listen to the radio: more music, news or live football. The rain had abated and the tourist decided to walk back all the way to his hotel, but before he had reached the middle of the bridge, the rain was suddenly strong again. There was no point in turning back now and he could not even see the taxis in the avalanche of cars passing by. He ducked his head between his shoulders and pressed forward. From the mosques on both sides of the straits rose the sorrowful voices of the muezzins.

He returned to his hotel, took a shower and changed. Then he took his laptop down to the lobby to use the wireless internet connection. He ordered black tea and a cognac and tried to focus in order to write his hotel review, but he found it difficult. He started the same sentence over and over again, then he read it several times and finally deleted it. At last, he closed his laptop, took a sip from his lukewarm tea and finished the cognac. He ordered another. He knew that if he gave up on writing the review now it would be even more difficult when he attempted it next. He opened the laptop and started again.

He could not think of anything else except a vapid retelling of the information contained in the brochures he found at the reception: a few good words about the location, the number and style of the hotel restaurants, the fantastic offers of the spa, etc. He wrote several sentences in the same vein, then he stopped and read them. Then he suddenly realised how he had to continue and began to write faster and faster, nodding to himself, without going back to read what he had already written. When he was finished, he ordered another cognac and sat back.

The review was monstrously vapid. Sentences such as "There are (...) rooms in the hotel that will make you feel at home" were conceived as a grotesque parody of the style in which hotel brochures were written. Between the lines should be read that this hotel was just as impersonal as the review about it. The tourist read it once again and sent it to the website before he had a chance to change his mind. Then he went up to his room and spent the rest of the day thinking about various apocalyptic scenarios for the end of this whole thing.

The next day, he ticked off several mosques and the underground reservoir with the cut-off stone head and returned to his hotel. He had called the girl's youth hostel as soon as he had woken up in the morning but they had told him that she had not arrived yet.

He went up to his room to take his laptop, went down to the lobby and sat in the same massive leather armchair that he had spent the whole previous afternoon sitting in. He opened his laptop and checked the tourist website first. His review was read and rated positively by a surprising number of visitors – either his sense of irony was not that difficult to get, or completely the opposite. The tourist shrugged, closed the tourist website and opened his profile in the other website. There was one new message from his client.

He looked up, found the waiter and ordered another cognac before he read it. The girl was writing to say that she was in fact not coming in Istanbul – hitch-hiking her way out of Ephesus, she had met some Bulgarian windsurfers driving back from some Turkish island and she was going to wait for him in a Sofia hotel from an international chain that he knew well.

The tourist carefully closed his profile, cut the wireless connection, switched off his laptop and closed it. The waiter brought him his cognac, the tourist gestured for him to wait, drank it off in one go and ordered another.

He hated waiting.

9. Bulgaria

The tourist did not understand people who made a mess. After he checked in a hotel, he always dedicated fifteen minutes to the task of taking all of his luggage out of his only bag and distributing it methodically between the wardrobe, the bathroom and the nightstand. He always left his things in the same places so he never had to look for them whenever he needed them. He did not even misplace the television remote because he always left it immediately in front of the television set after he had finished watching.

In a single night, the girl had made such a mess in their hotel room that in the morning she could not find her ChapStick and she emphatically refused to leave the hotel without it. For the first five minutes, he was unsuccessfully trying to help her; then he suggested that they could leave without it and buy another one from the first pharmacy that they saw on the street, but the girl explained to him that she bought her ChapStick from a single chain of natural products shops in the UK and she was absolutely positive that they would not find it in Sofia. The tourist sighed, switched off the television set, left the remote immediately in front of it and went to the window of the room to look outside.

He arrived in Sofia the previous night after ten hours on a bus which smelled like farm animals. The bus fought its way through an epic traffic jam along a boulevard running parallel to a canal with a sorry excuse for a river clogged with waste at the bottom, and stopped at a tiny, crowded station where most passengers had plastic bags for luggage. The tourist went out of the station and into the first car waiting on the taxi stop; the driver was smoking incessantly, loudly cursing all other drivers on the road and listening simultaneously to a radio station playing some kind of Oriental pop and the shocking crackling sounds produced by the dispatch system of the taxi company. The taxi pulled out of the bus station parking lot, made a U-turn and plunged right back into the same traffic jam which the tourist had endured on the way into the city. This time, the tourist was closer to the canal and he could see that there was not only waste on the banks of the river but also some kind of improvised stalls selling everyday items. On the whole, Sofia looked like a city in the Middle East but smaller.

The hotel was a crescent-shaped building facing a round square paved with yellow cobblestones. In the middle of the square was a statue of a horseman, but unfortunately it was facing the other way and all that could be seen from the hotel entrance was the horse's back end.

The girl was drinking dark ale in the lobby bar. The other customers were the same as in any other hotel bar from an international chain anywhere in the world: mostly men with their jackets off and their neckties loose, conscious of the few women in their company. The men were foreigners, usually on a business trip; the women were usually representatives of the local company, interpreters or escorts, and sometimes all three at once.

The girl smiled, kissed him on the cheek and led the way to reception where she checked in first, then she turned to him and handed him the key card for the room. It took him several seconds to realise that they were going to be in the same room.

Through the window of their room, he could see the round square with the yellow cobblestones and several interesting but badly maintained buildings. Viewed from up here, Sofia looked like Vienna but in the same way that the ancient Roman colonies in North Africa must have looked like Rome.

They walked out of the hotel, crossed the square and looked at an impressive Orthodox church with a golden dome and another square with an even more impressive Soviet-era monument featuring iron soldiers with sharp bayonets held up by iron women workers with downcast faces. The tourist remarked that they did not have to walk out of the hotel to see all that, because both the church and the monument were visible from the window of their room.

The girl had bought a guidebook and insisted on visiting some antique ruins so the tourist walked back alone, had lunch in the hotel restaurant and went up to the room. First he organised the desk, sorting the girl's things in one half of the desktop and his own, considerably fewer things, in the other. Then he sat down and opened his laptop to write the review about the hotel.

His idea was to compose it like a cooking recipe in which the necessary ingredients were the hard facts about the hotel, the manner of preparation were his notes on the staff and the service, and the serving suggestion was the description of the overall atmosphere on the streets of the Bulgarian capital. (Or at least those streets in the immediate vicinity of the hotel, as he did not even want to think about the boulevard from the previous day.) He browsed several popular cooking websites first to get a feeling of the style, then he opened a new file and typed up one of his more successful reviews in less than an hour. After he sent it to the tourist website, he had nothing else to do except go down to the lobby bar and get drunk.

He did not know what to do with this girl. Or rather, he did, he corrected himself a few drinks later, but he had given in to the impulse to postpone his decision and now it was getting more and more difficult to face. Perhaps they just needed to talk about it.

The girl came back very late, her hair smelled of marijuana and she was very excited when she started telling him some story about the incredible people that she had met in the park, but both of them lost interest in the story before it was finished. Then she accused him of being drunk, went into the bathroom, ran a bath and fell asleep in it. He tried to make her move to the bed but she refused to wake up. Since he did not trust himself to pick her up from the slippery bathtub and carry her into the room, the tourist waited a little longer, brushed his teeth and went to bed. He did not hear her come out of the bathroom, but when he woke up in the morning the girl was next to him in the bed.

While they were having breakfast, she told him about her plan for the day: they were to rent a car and drive east, to a small town in the central part of the country which had been the country's capital in some long gone historical period. She showed him photographs of the town in her guidebook: it looked like any medieval European town (scattered on several hills with a river snaking through them, with something like a castle on top of one hill), but with less colour and character. He left her at the reception to take care of the rental car and went up to the room where he was surprised to learn that there was, in fact, one hotel in this town which was on the waiting list of the tourist website. The tourist reserved a room in the hotel for one night.

His stomach churned when he thought about the rental car. The tourist was not a good driver since he very rarely used cars to go from one place to another, and something told him that he would not like the driving etiquette in Bulgaria. The girl soon came up to the room and perkily announced that their car will be waiting outside the hotel entrance in thirty minutes. The tourist cautiously inquired if the girl had a driving license but the girl just laughed, exactly as he had expected.

The car was Korean and it was enormous, more like a minivan. When he climbed in the driver's seat he felt like he was on the bridge of a ship. Naturally, it had a manual transmission. At least it had a navigation system – the tourist thought that if it did not have a navigation system, he would have flatly refused to sit behind the wheel.

He carefully started driving along the front of the hotel, guided by the soft female voice of the navigation system. The car jumped every time he changed gears, and moved inexplicably slowly. There was some kind of symbol blinking in red on the dashboard. When they stopped at the first corner, the tourist noticed a sharp burning smell and clouds of smoke roiling up from under the bonnet. Another car stopped on their left and the two young men inside it started pointing energetically towards the bonnet of their car, as if the tourist could not see that it was smoking.

They painfully reached the other side of the street and he pulled over as soon as he could. The girl kept voicing various possible explanations for the car's behaviour, most of which seemed irrational, so he asked her to stop. He turned off the engine, waited a little and turned it back on. This was clearly enough for the navigation system to forget what they had programmed into it, so that now he would not know where to drive even if they managed to set off properly. The tourist cautiously stepped on the gas and the car lurched forward but something was interfering with its motion and when they stopped at the next light, the smoke coming out from under the bonnet was much thicker, black and suffocating.

His face turned red. He did not know what to do. The girl silently opened the glove compartment, rummaged around in the car papers and came up with a user manual as thick as a paperback novel. The tourist pulled over again and turned off the engine. Curious faces were turning to look back at them in the cars passing by.

Without saying a word, the girl reached for the key to start the engine again. The tourist started to protest but she glanced at the manual and then pressed a big red button at the base of the manual transmission stick. Then she nodded to him. He released the clutch and stepped on the gas pedal. The car shot forward. The acceleration blew off the smoke and the burning smell. The girl smiled with satisfaction, tossed the user manual back into the glove compartment and banged it shut. The tourist's face turned an even brighter shade of red when he realised that he had been trying to drive without releasing the hand brake.

Most of the old capital turned out to be repulsive apartment blocks from the nineteen seventies but their hotel was in the historical quarter and it was unexpectedly good. It had only twelve rooms and the tourist had reserved room number eleven, on the top floor. Their balcony looked on low hills dotted with small houses, churches and the faux-medieval castle that he had already seen in the photographs in the guidebook.

After they had seen the historical quarter with the narrow alleys, the steep stairs and the tiny workshops with frowning artisans working away, there was not much to do so they returned to the hotel and had sex. As they lay on the bed afterwards, the girl was playing with the light switch and she suddenly offered to help him with the review for this hotel. The tourist did not mind and the girl jumped up from the bed, bursting with energy.

She started by walking around the whole room, the bathroom and the balcony, then she put on a bathrobe and walked out into the corridor and finally went down to the reception, all the time taking photographs with her mobile phone: close-ups of the lighting fixtures, the furniture, the cup for the toothbrushes in the bathroom and the envelopes on the table next to the television set. Then she asked to use his laptop, transferred all the photographs from her phone to the laptop, browsed around in the programmes, talking under her breath, and switched on a programme for formatting comic strips that the tourist had never used.

Two hours later, in which he watched television, read a book and even managed to take a nap, the girl nudged him on the shoulder to wake him up and proudly displayed the result of her work: she had put together a comic strip from her photographs in which the inanimate objects from the hotel were communicating with each other in speech bubbles. The tourist had to admit that it was pretty clever: the various pieces of furniture, lamps and so on were depicted as weary, jaded stoics mired in incessant intrigue behind each other's backs. The hotel itself was just the backdrop of the action – the same way in which the exotic locations all over the world were the background of the exploits of the secret agent in the film that he had had to watch so many times. There was nothing left for him to do but send the review to the tourist website and take the girl out to dinner.

When they returned to the hotel the receptionist explained in faltering but friendly English that tonight they would have the chance to watch the special light show projected from the hill with the castle that this town was famous for. They just had to walk out on the balcony of their room to see it. The tourist asked for a bottle of wine to be brought up to their room.

While they were watching the lights, he asked her what they were going to do next. The girl replied matter-of-factly that she wanted to see the sea before she died. The tourist did not say anything more.

They finished the wine and went to bed. Their sex was getting better and better.

After breakfast on the next day, they drove on east and in a few hours reached a big town on the coast that the girl's guidebook called "the sea capital of Bulgaria". Just like the actual capital and the old capital that they had seen, the sea capital was mostly concrete apartment blocks and the rest looked like something the tourist had already seen elsewhere, only smaller and grubbier. The guidebook claimed that the local archaeological museum exhibited the most ancient gold articles in human history, but the archaeological museum was closed so they drove on north until they reached one of the seaside resorts. (On the previous evening, when the tourist opened the tourist website to see how the comic strip was doing – it was doing pretty well – he had a rare message from his editor; the manager of a hotel on the beach in the seaside resort who was obviously an avid fan of the tourist website had contacted them asking for his hotel to be included in the "ongoing survey of Bulgarian tourist attractions". The tourist shuddered but accepted the job.)

The hotel was shaped like a horseshoe facing the sea. Their balcony on the fourth floor looked on the deep blue eye of the round pool inside the horseshoe and the beach reserved for the guests of the hotel. The tourist did not mind staying in such hotels, cut off from the outside world and completely self-sufficient, encouraging their guests to stay on the property at all times.

The girl had already changed into her bathing suit and she was busy applying sunscreen. The tourist did not manage to fight off the thought that the use of sunscreen by a person determined to commit suicide shortly afterwards was somewhat superfluous. He told her that he was tired and he would stay in the room, so she went outside by herself. In a few minutes, he saw her – she came out of the inside entrance of the hotel, walked by the pool and continued towards the beach and the sea.

He studied the contents of the minibar and opened a beer. Then he sat on the balcony and looked outside, where he could see other hotel guests. Their voices – children screaming and laughing and, less often, the raised voice of an adult – were muffled by the distance and he could not discern any words.

Between the edge of the balcony and the edge of the pool, four floors down, there were five or six metres of empty space and then terracotta tiles – it was enough for someone to smash to their death if they happened to fall off the balcony. From the sea came the distant roar of the surf and he could see the red flag on the beach flapping wildly against the backdrop of the white crests on the waves – it was enough for someone to drown if they happened to swim too far in.

He had another beer, then he switched on his laptop and spent the next hour writing a hotel review in the voice of an anonymous killer hired by people who wanted to kill themselves, travelling all over the world under the disguise of a hotel review writer. The hotel was described from the point of view of a man who was professionally obsessed with looking for suitable spots to stage a fatal accident – the bathtub, the emergency staircase, the steps leading down to the pool. Then he selected the whole text, deleted it and sat looking at the empty screen of his laptop until he heard the distinctive sounds of the girl's flip-flops approaching down the corridor.

She returned, kissed him on the cheek and sat on the balcony to be out of his way while he was working. He thought for a minute, then he wrote a new review – in the form of a cocktail recipe in which the necessary ingredients were the hard facts about the hotel, the manner of preparation were his notes on the staff and the room, and the serving suggestion was the overall atmosphere on the Bulgarian coast. (Or at least what he could see from the balcony.) He sent it off without reading it and suggested to the girl to get dressed for dinner. He needed alcohol.

They sat in the hotel restaurant and the tourist ordered a bottle of wine with the food and another one when it was finished. When they had come in, the restaurant had been empty, then it had quickly filled up with other guests – sunburnt, displaying too much flesh, shouting in different languages – and then it had gradually emptied once again. The tourist ordered another bottle. They were sitting outside where they could see the sea and the air was filled with the scent of salt and seaweeds.

The girl called the waiter and asked that the last bottle of wine be brought up to their room. In the elevator, the tourist was slightly swaying. They went inside the room without switching on the lights. The breeze came through the open balcony door and made the curtains roll like waves. The tourist crashed down on the bed. In a few minutes, two waiters appeared at the door with a trolley carrying a bucket of ice with their bottle of wine inside. The girl thanked them and closed the door.

He was already falling asleep but she patiently woke him up so that they could have sex. This time it went on and on and finally she (face down on the bed, with her red face pressed against the pillow) was sobbing and almost inarticulately repeating please, please, please as he (clutching her with his knuckles gone white, panting with the effort) was shoving himself harder and harder into her body trying to come.

In the morning, the girl was still sleeping deeply when the tourist carefully sneaked out of bed, dressed, put his luggage back into his bag and closed it without using the zipper so as not to wake her up. He left without turning back and he closed the door very slowly – he had noticed on the previous day that the mechanism made a very loud noise when it clicked into place. Then he walked down the corridor to the elevator. It was very early and it was completely quiet in the hotel. No one could be seen except a few cleaners who were moving, ant-like, among the lounging chairs by the pool.

The elevator arrived and the door opened with a ping, but the tourist did not enter and in a few seconds the door closed once again. It had a matt metal finish and he could see his reflection only as a faceless silhouette. He stayed for a while in front of the elevator, then he turned and walked back to the room where the girl was sleeping, to finish the job.

10. The U.S.A.

The tourist considered most tourist attractions repulsive, especially in the U.S.A. where any tourist attraction seemed to come with a well-organised ticket line, heavy security with dogs and metal detectors and a one-hour wait, only to see something that one had already seen much better looking on the internet. After he squeezed himself together with a dozen others into the elevator of the only historical skyscraper open for visitors and he rode up to the top floor in an atmosphere of impatience and vague unease, he was met with a crammed souvenir shop and the flash of a hundred cameras – as usual, the tourists were taking their photographs in front of anything that stood in their way.

The client did not take his photograph. Instead, the young man with the baseball cap and the backpack – looking American to the bone, even a little out of place among the tourists from all over the world – went out on the roof with a view towards Manhattan and stood there for almost thirty minutes, rapt by the skyline, checking which building was which in his guidebook, dropping coins in the telescopes and chatting up the tourists walking by to share his excitement.

When he finally came back inside, the tourist discreetly followed him to the elevator, out of the building and down the broad sidewalks of the famous avenues, to the legendary central park. The client arrived there at five in the afternoon, just like the day before, and just like the day before, he started jogging along the park alleys in the growing dusk. The snow was cleared off the alleys and piled to the sides where it had long ago changed its white for unpleasant shades of gray and yellow, but it was still very cold – gusts of vapour were coming out of the client's mouth as he jogged by the hot dog stand where the tourist was standing, vapour rose from his own mouth, open to receive the hot dog, as well as from the hot dog itself.

An hour later it was completely dark and even colder. The client walked down into the subway and rode the same line from the same station as the day before. The tourist decided that there was no point in following him, because he knew where the young man was going – to his hotel, a few blocks away from the boulevard where the theatres were. Instead, the tourist hailed a taxi, managed to explain to the driver where he wanted to go even though the man did not speak any English and behaved like it was his first time in New York and also in a car, and returned to his own hotel in the winter night.

The hotel was a member of a chain of small luxury hotels all over the world which offered exquisite service and the highest standards in an authentic atmosphere. The tourist read this in the catalogue that he found at the reception and carried up to his room. Then he opened his laptop and worked on his review for several hours, using historical websites to research what buildings had stood in the same spot in New York for the past two hundred years. The theme of the review was the fact that this hotel offered its guests the rare possibility – at least in the U.S.A. – to steep themselves in tradition without leaving their rooms. After he sent the review, he opened the minibar, turned up the air conditioning and switched on the television set.

At five on the following afternoon, he was already in the central park wearing sporting clothes, gloves and trainers, as if he was out to jog. He also wore a ski-mask on his face to protect himself from the cold air, as well as a knitted cap, and in the pocket of his jacket he carried the telescoping baton that he had purchased freely from the same sporting equipment store where he had bought all the rest.

The client had a knitted cap, too. The tourist waited for the young man to jog by, pretending to stretch next to a bench, then gave him a fifty metre start and started running after him. When they entered the park and the dusk deepened, he shortened the distance. There was no one else on the alleys. The plan of the tourist was to emulate a robbery gone fatal – the situation did not look improbable at all on a winter's evening in New York's central park which had a long history of similar crimes.

He caught up with the client next to a tree by the alley. The young man was propped up against the tree, bent over to stretch the muscles in his back, with his eyes on the ground, and his breath was coming out of his mouth in great gusts of vapour. Without slowing down, the tourist veered off the alley, ran towards him, took the baton out of his pocket, opened it with a single outwards swing (he had practiced all morning until he was sure that he accomplished the same result every time), approached the client and brought down the baton on his head with all of his strength.

There was an absurd cracking noise and the baton bounced off the young man's knitted cap with such force that it almost hit the tourist in the face. The young man nimbly jumped away, turned around and laughed when he saw the stunned expression on his attacker's face. Then he shook his finger at him playfully, as if the tourist was a child who had tried to do something mischievous instead of attempted murder. Finally, he took off his knitted cap to reveal the bicycle helmet that he was wearing under it, and sprinted off through the park in the darkness, laughing all the way.

The tourist stayed by the tree, breathing heavily and trying to comprehend what had just happened. He pressed the tip of the baton against the tree to retract it to the closed position and threw it in a garbage bin. It was already completely dark in the park and he turned to walk back to the subway station. The night was not a success as it was, but it would have been a disaster if someone had decided to attack himself.

When he returned to the hotel and opened his laptop, he had one new message sent to his profile on the other website. It was sent by the young man who had escaped in the park and it contained just two (or was it three?) words: "you're it".

Washington was bright and sunny but so cold that people's breath rushed through condensation straight into a cloud of ice crystals shimmering in the sunlight. The tourist stayed in a private residence in an expensive suburb, owned by a gay couple of lawyers. One floor of their house was rented out to visitors under a particularly innovative scheme and a percentage of the income financed various charities. The house was on three floors, with a sauna and a small gym in the basement, and it was as elegantly furnished as could be expected. The lawyers were white and Latin American, fifty and forty, respectively, dressed beyond reproach and cooked with flair and gusto. The rent was exorbitant but it was already paid for by the tourist website and the tourist spent an uneventful evening with his hosts, ate an extraordinary dinner and drank almost two bottles of wine before he retired to his room. He had recorded his conversation with the couple, so he switched on his laptop and edited the recording down to an interview which described the innovative scheme and sketched the character of the two hosts in a rather positive light.

After that, he opened his profile on the other website but there was nothing new: the client had already informed him that he would be in an unnecessarily expensive café from a famous international chain from ten until eleven on the following morning. The tourist switched off his laptop and went to bed but his expectations for a quiet night were miscalculated: he had eaten too much and he turned in his bed for hours on end, while the whole house around him creaked and popped from the arctic temperature outside.

On the next day, the sun was shining brightly but it was so cold that the local radio and television stations broadcast an official warning to all Washington, D.C., residents to stay indoors unless absolutely necessary. Weather reports ended with information about temperatures on the U.S. east coast but they were in Fahrenheit and when the tourist tried to figure them out in the Celsius degrees that he was used to, the resulting numbers were too improbable and he decided that he had made a mistake.

Twenty minutes after nine, he was already in the café, seated at a window table. In front of him, there was a large cup containing a complicated coffee beverage with milk, cream and various flavours running to a preposterous total cost, and an open laptop, much like in front of every other customer at every other table.

His client arrived at ten minutes to ten, riding a motorcycle. The motorcycle was manufactured in Japan but the model was such a classic that it would not have looked out of place on any American highway. The young man was wearing a fringed leather jacket and he had no helmet, favouring a bandana headband and mirrored sunglasses instead. He had a three-day stubble shimmering with frost. The tourist thought that if the client kept riding a motorcycle in this weather, he would not have to do anything else except wait for the man to catch a cold that would kill him. The client slowly rode his motorcycle past the café and took a turn round the corner to park it. A minute later, he walked into the café, ordered a coffee and sat down in the corner to drink it, keeping his sunglasses on.

The tourist browsed several motorcycling websites using the wireless internet connection in the café, closed his laptop, took a last sip from his coffee beverage and walked out. The motorcycle was parked several metres down the side street, next to a dumpster. Although the morning was bright, the side street, running like a narrow canyon between the tall cold buildings, was deep in shadow. The tourist looked back to make sure that no one was watching him, put his gloves on, crouched next to the motorcycle on the side of the dumpster and took out a fruit knife that he had stolen from the lawyers' kitchen. When he was finished, he threw the knife in the dumpster and slowly walked on down the side street until he reached the next corner. He took a right, walked one more block, took another right and walked until he was back on the boulevard with the café which he crossed, walked a little more to the right and found another café, situated almost directly opposite the café from the international chain. This was a very different establishment – the Greek national flag was hoisted above the door, there were only three tables which were not exceptionally clean and the coffee was strong and bitter, served in tiny cups with nothing else at all. The tourist ordered a grilled cheese sandwich to go with his coffee and bought the fattest local newspaper.

At five minutes past eleven, the client walked out of the café on the other side of the street, looked around and made for the side street where his motorcycle was parked. A minute later, he appeared at the corner, paused for a few seconds, made a prohibited left turn across the boulevard and accelerated, going past the Greek café. The growl of the engine made the windows rattle.

The tourist followed him with his eyes over the newspaper as the young man raced for the street lights at the next corner, missed the green light, tried to brake, his brakes malfunctioned, his motorcycle kept going forward, he abruptly turned the front wheel, the motorcycle skidded sideways, the young man flew off the motorcycle in front of the cars, the motorcycle crashed against the curb on the other side of the intersection, leaped up into the air, flipped over and crashed back on the street in a cascade of sparks.

There were shouts and screams from the pedestrians, screeching of car tyres and heavy impacts of metal against metal when the cars from the two crossing streets decelerated in a series of crashes. The tourist quickly walked out of the café together with the owner and the rest of the customers to see what was going on.

There were several cars at odd angles to one another in the middle of the intersection – the front bumpers of some had deformed the back bumpers or the doors of others. A small crowd was already there – drivers and pedestrians ready to offer help or impatient to see. The tourist approached, straining to see among the people.

The first thing he saw was the bandana on his head. Miraculously, the young man had not even lost his mirrored sunglasses. He was standing in the middle of the crowd, shaking his head, then he raised his hands to show everyone that he was okay and he smiled. Some of the people applauded him.

The new message from the client said that he was not in any way to blame for the continued failure of the "operation" (this was the actual word that he had used, as if he was a character in a film). Since his motorcycle was smashed, he was going to have to take the bus. This was all.

The tourist waited for him at the bus station. The young man gave him a crooked smile when he appeared. The tourist did not smile back. The client bought a ticket to Philadelphia, and the tourist – who was waiting in line two people back – bought the same ticket, paying in cash.

They were on the highway when the east coast was finally overrun by the gigantic snowstorm that the weather reports had warned about for the past several days. There were numerous car accidents which caused traffic jams along the highway and they were running several hours late. The tourist was so furious at the client already that he fantasised about following him into the horrible bathroom of the bus terminal when they finally arrived and slamming his head against the sink, but he had to admit that if the young man decided to fight back, things would probably go the other way round.

The driver of the bus to Philadelphia was a big black woman with a fantastic hairdo who kept turning around and cracking jokes to the passengers on her microphone. The tourist gloomily thought that considering the U.S. government's record of rescue operations, if the driver lost control over the bus and they crashed, all of them would probably freeze to death on the highway and in this way his job would finally be completed.

The moment they arrived at the bus station in Philadelphia, the young man jumped out of the bus, hoisting his backpack on the run, and sprinted for the row of taxis waiting in front. The tourist cursed under his breath and followed him, pushing his way through the crowd in the waiting room. The young man threw a glance back over his shoulder and jumped into the first taxi. The tourist saw him gesticulating furiously to the taxi driver to make him leave immediately. A few seconds later the car shot out of its place, throwing snow and slush behind, and pushed into the traffic on the street, greeted with honking horns. The tourist finally managed to get out of the building and looked at the taxi speeding away. He could have boarded the next taxi in line and told the driver to follow that car, but it seemed to be going too far. After all, he was working for a website which organised suicides, not car chases. He shook his head and made to turn back into the waiting room to decide what to do next.

At this moment, the taxi with the young man inside drove straight through the red light at the end of the street, skidded on the snow in the intersection which had not been cleared yet, took a spin (the tourist vaguely remembered something he had read in a guidebook about the U.S.A. – unlike Europeans, Americans tended not to use different car tyres in summer and winter), and came directly in front of an eight-wheeler which was rushing into the intersection from the street opposite and blasting its horn, as powerful as that of a ship. The truck smashed into the side of the taxi with such force that the car was thrown up in the air, took a half flip and crashed back on the street on its roof. The driver of the truck had already started turning, trying to avoid the car, but he still hit it once more passing by so that the car started spinning on its roof like a toy. The people on the sidewalk next to the tourist had frozen in place with their mouths open, looking at the scene with shock and horror.

The tourist sighed with relief and went back into the heated waiting room.

11. Berlin

The tourist was not impressed by Berlin. In every single issue of the airlines' board magazines that he always read from the first page to the last in order to avoid thinking about the possibility of unexpected turbulence because of which all passengers were advised to keep their seatbelts on during the whole flight, there was at least one author who expressed the common opinion that Berlin was the city of the moment where everything interesting was happening right now. The tourist did not share this opinion. He thought that Berlin was the same too big and disorganised, dirty and anonymous city it had always been, ever since the cold war. Every time a city was proclaimed to be the city of the moment – Tokyo, Moscow, Buenos Aires – the tourist was invariably disappointed by it.

The transoceanic flight landed in Munich. The tourist did not mind Munich. He had been there in the summer and he was left with the impression that the city was more Italian than German. He had spent quite some time in the "English Garden", as they called their central park, and he wanted to see it again in winter. But he was still at the airport in Munich, drinking cappuccino and browsing the tourist website to find a suitable hotel to review, when he received a new message sent to his profile – it was a suggestion by his editor to review a large hotel from an international chain which was located in Berlin. The tourist checked the flights of low-cost airlines and managed to reserve a seat on a flight which left in two hours, so he unhurriedly finished his cappuccino, checked in and spent the rest of the time in a bookshop trying to choose a paperback novel, finally giving up and buying a tiny guidebook for Berlin which listed just ten top tourist attractions instead.

He arrived in the German capital at noon, took a taxi to the hotel, checked in, unpacked and immediately went back outside, taking only his new guidebook. The end of the year was approaching and there were Christmas markets everywhere, garlands of blinking lights and a holiday atmosphere: hysterical children high on hot chocolate, high-coloured fathers who had been guzzling mulled wine since morning, high-strung mothers weighted down by presents for the whole family. The tourist visited six of the ten attractions listed in the guidebook before he lost interest. The author's selection was quite unorthodox – it seemed that the single requirement for including an attraction in the guidebook was for it to be located in an especially windy place open on all sides and/or in a rundown neighbourhood crammed full of immigrants, defaced with graffiti and sound tracked by Oriental music spilling out of the grocery stores and barber shops.

He returned to the hotel, went up to his room and drank several of the tiny bottles of alcohol that he found in the minibar. Then he took a shower, shaved, changed and called reception to ask for his clothes to be picked up for washing. Finally, feeling that he had done everything that had to be done, he went down to the lobby, sat at the bar and ordered a whisky and soda before dinner.

Two seats away was a woman his age, focused on her laptop, sipping her cocktail delicately but often. She was very tall, with very short ash-blonde hair, and she would have been beautiful if she was not so thin. She was wearing an elegant black pantsuit and shoes that looked more like men's footwear. In addition, she was sitting like a man – her feet were planted on the rungs of the two bar stools to the left and to the right of her – and the tourist noticed the deep scar crawling out from under her left trouser leg and into her black sock.

Never taking her eyes off the computer screen, the woman explained that the scar was left from the bite of a stray dog. She spoke English with a German or Austrian accent. The tourist was embarrassed and tried to apologise for his curiosity but the woman closed her laptop, turned to him and smiled before she assured him that it was okay. She was a manager in an advertising agency which had clients in some former Soviet countries, and during a business trip she had decided to see for herself the production facilities of a brewery, hoping to get some inspiration for their upcoming advertising campaign. When she got out of the company car in the parking lot of the brewery on the outskirts of a former Soviet city with an unpronounceable name, the stray dog in question furiously attacked her and tried to rip her apart.

Her cocktail was finished, the tourist nodded in question at her empty glass, the woman nodded in agreement and he caught the bartender's eye to order one more of the same for each of them.

Next came the inevitable question about his own profession. The tourist gave the usual answer, hoping to get it over quickly, but instead she asked him a few more, very relevant questions about the way the tourist website was organised and the kind of contracts it made with the hotel chains. While they were talking, the woman was frowning in concentration, sipping her cocktail in tiny business-like sips, as if she had decided to focus all of her mental capacity on the conversation after she had finished her work for the day. The tourist moved to sit next to her. When they finished their drinks, she ordered one more of the same for each of them.

They had dinner together in the hotel restaurant. The woman ordered a salad from the menu and asked the waiter to repeat all the ingredients that she did not want in her salad, as well as those that she wanted them to be replaced with. Clearly, she did not eat most things that people thought of as food. On the other hand, she had no problem with drinking. The tourist was relieved to let her order the wine after she opened the wine list and studied it with the expression of a person who knows what she is doing, and they shared two bottles of some light white wine from the valley of the Rhine. When they were finished with the second bottle, there was no one else in the restaurant.

They went out of the restaurant back into the hotel lobby and the woman walked in front in the direction of the elevators, without turning to say goodbye or goodnight to him. The tourist followed her. They entered the elevator together. The woman reached and pressed the button for her floor. They arrived in silence. The elevator door opened and the woman got out. He got out as well. They went together to the door of her room. The woman opened the door. The tourist went inside. The woman followed him inside and closed the door.

When they started kissing, the woman took his head with her two hands, as if she wished to navigate him in her mouth. They fell down on the bed and impatiently took their clothes off. The scar reached up almost to her knee. He tried to kiss it but the woman pulled him up. She treated sex in the same methodical, efficient way as she did everything else. Afterwards, they lay next to each other for a while, and then the woman abruptly stood up and walked into the bathroom. She left the door opened while she used the toilet, then she entered the shower and started brushing her teeth at the same time. The tourist listened to her for a little longer, then he stood up and started to put his clothes back on.

When he passed by the bathroom door, the woman appeared, wrapped in the hotel bathrobe. Her wet hair was sticking out. In the bright light, with her make-up washed away, she looked younger and older at the same time. She explained to him that she had to leave early the next morning. He nodded. The woman smiled and said goodnight. He said goodnight as well and returned to his room where he found his clothes – washed, dried, ironed and folded on the bed.

After breakfast, the tourist sat down in the lobby bar once again, ordered a latte and opened his laptop. He wanted to describe the large international hotel as a tiny part of a huge invisible structure of people and resources, towering behind every seemingly simple thing accepted by the guests as something natural – the delivery of eggs and oranges for breakfast, for example, or the cleaning of hundreds of rooms that had to be vacant at this precise moment. He visited several websites on military history, thinking to give hotel managers equivalent ranks from the Wehrmacht, but he changed his mind and replaced them with the more neutral military ranks of NATO. The end result was a little dry but very informative – he had a bottomless reserve of observations about the functioning of a hotel system and he had never used them as the basis for a review. When he was finished, he read the text once again, made some small changes, felt satisfied with the result and sent it off to the tourist website before he closed his laptop.

The young man that he had last seen in the crashed taxi in Philadelphia was sitting on the opposite table. He had a plaster on his temple and one hand in a sling, but otherwise he seemed to be just fine, wearing a business suit and sipping an espresso with his good hand. The tourist kept staring at him while the client stood up, walked to his table and sat down with a serene smile on his face.

His first words were that the game was not over. He had paid for this and he had no intention of accepting no for an answer until they had reached the end. The tourist asked him how he had found him in Berlin. The client smiled even more brightly and explained that the tourist's visit in Berlin was not coincidental at all. The order to review this particular hotel was sent to his personal profile on the tourist website but the young man claimed that the hotel managers did not even know about this. Still smiling, the client told him that he had made his first million in the software industry where he had made waves with a new networking management algorithm, so it had been child's play for him to hack the tourist website and send the fake message.

The tourist stared at the holiday decoration behind the bar. The little lamps were doing the only thing they were made to do – blinking on and off. The young man kept talking. He had ordered a suicide for himself not because he wanted to die, but because he wanted to live – to taste life on the edge where each minute could be his last and thus much more precious for it. And so on. The tourist waved to the waiter and ordered schnapps even though it was eleven in the morning. He had already traversed half of the U.S. east coast playing hide-and-seek with this young man and he found it difficult to be infected by his enthusiasm.

The client sat closer to him to tell him about his next idea. He had chanced upon the story of the legendary fencing societies which had flourished in Germany during the nineteenth century. The duels, fought to first blood, had been – according to the young man's sources, whatever they were – an obligatory part of every young man's education, and the scars they left – usually on the face – were indispensable for a good standing in social life. The young man had managed to get hold of a private fencing club which unofficially kept this tradition alive, and he had reserved a piste and weapons for this afternoon.

The tourist finished his drink and nodded. Of course, he was prepared to meet the client's wish to end his life in the way that he saw fit. This was the only presentable answer, given the circumstances. He enquired after the exact address of the fencing club and carefully wrote it down. Then he left the young man in the lobby bar, went up to his room and opened the websites of the German railways and the Berlin airport at the same time.

He absolutely needed to get out of this city on the first plane or train that he could find.

12. Amsterdam

The tourist was terrified by the idea that someone could track him. His entire life was defined by anonymity, unpredictability and constant motion. Which is why, when he glimpsed the familiar silhouette of the young man reflected in a shop window on the street leading from Amsterdam central station to the centre of the city, his instinctive reaction was to run, to hide, to burrow underground. He walked into the first hotel that he saw – a narrow building with an Arab diner on the first floor and a creaking wooden staircase leading past it – checked himself in and paid in advance for two nights. The price was an unpleasant surprise. The owner of the hotel seemed to think that it was all about the location and there was no need to factor in the quality of the services that he offered. The tourist got the key for his room, glanced outside through the window of the Arab diner – the young man could no longer be seen – and walked up to the third floor to leave his luggage.

The hotel was disgusting. His room was small and so irregularly shaped that the vestibule – for which he had no use – was larger than the other half of the room where his bed was. The only window leaked icy air and looked on something like a shaft down the inside of the building, dark and stinking of moisture. The bathroom was lined with horrible greenish tiles – the tourist thought that he had seen them only in those films in which the protagonist ended up in the basement of the sinister secret police to be tortured – and cramped with a farcical bathtub with yellowed enamel and rusty iron feet in the shape of lion paws. (Or badger paws, there was no way to be sure.)

He put his bag on the bed and sat down next to it without taking his coat off. It was not warm in the room. Outside, it was a bright morning but inside everything was swimming in a sickly dusk.

The tourist took out his laptop but he did not open it. The young man who had ordered his own suicide but refused to die had mentioned his computer skills. If he was able to manipulate the order for a hotel review which had sent the tourist to Berlin, he was surely able to track him by the online reservation for the international train that the tourist had escaped on. The tourist had never attempted to contact people who could fix him with fake identification documents or credit cards – he had always considered this an unnecessary expense and something which would have increased the risk of unwanted attention from law enforcement rather than deflecting it. But then again, no one had ever tracked him in this manner. This cat-and-mouse game in which their roles were constantly changing was not at all to his liking.

The tourist sighed, took his laptop, walked out of the room, locked the door, took the stairs down by the Arab diner, walked out in the street, put on his sunglasses and looked around. In reality, there was only one way to end this game. He had to finish the job.

He walked along the main street until he found a coffee shop which offered wireless internet connection and actually sold coffee instead of marijuana. He took a seat inside and wrote a review about the hotel that he had checked in. The review was a list of fifty other hotels in Amsterdam which were better than this one – with a single sentence about each hotel detailing the way in which it was better. Many of them offered better value for money; almost all of them were cleaner and better lit; some were in even older but carefully maintained buildings; and there were a few with an even more central location. The tourist had stayed in some of the hotels that he wrote about, so he wrote from experience, and as for the rest, he collected the necessary information from tourist websites and forums. He sent his review, closed the laptop and put his sunglasses back on. He was sitting at a small table next to the window and he could see the central street. He had checked in the terrible hotel by chance, without an online reservation, so the client could not know any more about him than the fact that he had travelled by train and the time of his arrival. The only move for the young man would be to hover near the station until the tourist showed up, and this street was the most direct and obvious route into downtown Amsterdam. The tourist only had to wait – and then hope that he was more accomplished than the young man in the good old physical tailing on foot.

The young man appeared on the opposite sidewalk after forty-five minutes. He had already managed to buy himself a souvenir tee shirt with a huge smiling marijuana leaf that he was wearing under his leather jacket. The tourist left a banknote in the saucer with the bill and walked out of the café.

The client made for the red lights district but did not reach further than the canal which separated it from the historical centre and was densely dotted with little shops selling marijuana and hallucinogenic drugs. The weather was unseasonably mild and after he spent ten minutes in one of the shops, the young man sat on the bench in front, painted with enthusiasm but little skill to depict smiling mushrooms and aliens. He had bought an extravagantly long and thick hand-made cigarette – more of a cigar, really – that he smoked by himself and with obvious pleasure, watching the boats in the canal and the tourists on the opposite bank. The tourist was doubtful that in this condition the client would be able to recognise him, much less try to escape, but he still kept his distance, leaning on the railing of a bridge a hundred metres away, pretending first to take photographs and then to enjoy the sun.

The next stop of the client was a disgusting sex-theatre at the edge of the red lights district, advertised by both gigantic neon letters on the roof and an extraordinarily big black man wearing a purple tuxedo and tall hat who stood outside the entrance and stopped passers-by to describe the incredible spectacle inside. The young man talked to him for a while, laughing loudly and making a show of his disbelief, then he bought a ticket and wobbled in. The tourist reluctantly paid the giant in the tuxedo and followed the young man.

The theatre was a long narrow room with seats that the tourist preferred not to look at too closely. He could not have anyway as the room was submerged in bluish semi-darkness only partially dispersed by the reddish semi-darkness of the stage. All the seats were taken by men – most of them in noisy groups shouting encouragingly to each other in various British accents. The young man was seated in the front row, already completely integrated with his fellow spectators. The tourist sat in the back row.

After a while, some sentimental rock anthem started playing from the speakers and the stage was taken by a very ordinary girl with drooping breasts and a tired face. She smiled for the audience which burst in applause, then she performed a striptease.

For her next performance, the same girl brought out a chair from the wings, sat on it and, after some procrastination, spread her legs and started to masturbate, pretending to climax several times. The spectators took it even better than the previous act, encouraging the girl with applause and offering to give her a hand themselves. The girl looked like she had already heard all possible offers.

For the next performance, the girl was joined onstage by a man dressed as a gorilla. It was obviously a comic act because the gorilla explained to the audience that one of them must volunteer to come up on stage and assist the gorilla while the gorilla performed some complicated action involving the girl and a banana. Naturally, the client expressed the greatest enthusiasm and the gorilla chose him. The young man clambered up on the stage, happy to participate.

The tourist went outside to wait for him there.

In the deepening night, secretive black men had materialised on street corners, muttering offers for other concoctions in addition to the expansive range of drugs sold legally in the shops. After the client walked out of the sex-theatre, it was only a question of time before he stopped next to one of these men and procured something that he most probably used on the spot. The tourist listlessly followed him into the red lights district, beginning to hope that perhaps the young man would succeed in offing himself by the morning and the tourist would not have to do anything more to assist him.

The red lights district looked like a cheap kitschy enactment of one of those medieval paintings that warned against the danger of eternal damnation, always hovering over those seduced by the flesh. Flesh was everywhere: hundreds of sweating tourists were bustling along the narrow streets, dazed by alcohol and drugs, looking around with glazed eyes and licking their dry lips, and on both sides of the streets were uninterrupted rows of tiny booths, each housing one or two women in their underwear, usually black, who were trying to lure the tourists inside. When they succeeded, the man disappeared into the booth, sent off with encouraging shouts and whistles by his friends, and a curtain fell on him. The tourist could not comprehend how anyone managed to get an erection while merry crowds kept walking by less than two metres away. He could not even use the urinals in public toilets because he needed the solitude of the booth to do what he had come to do. But the young man that he was tailing clearly did not have the same problem – he walked in with one of the first women who waved to him and stayed inside for about fifteen minutes.

The night continued in the same vein. The tourist bought a caffeinated drink in a can to keep awake. The client looked unnaturally awake and incredibly inebriated at the same time, but he obviously had energy to spare as he visited one more booth and one more bar, this one selling marijuana cookies. About three in the morning, when they had left the red lights district behind and the tourist had fallen back a little even though the young man would have probably not noticed him even if the tourist had been walking directly in front of him, the client decided to relieve himself in a canal.

The tourist looked around. The façades of the houses around him were dark. He could not see any other people on the street. There were a few boat houses anchored in the canal, but they were dark and silent too.

The tourist picked up his pace. The young man was standing on the very edge of the canal, next to an anchored boat, swaying on his feet, murmuring something to himself and rotating this way and that as if he wanted to draw something with the stream of urine in the black water between the bank and the boat.

The tourist approached him at a run. The young man only heard him when he was a few steps away and tried to turn around, but he lost his balance and waved his arms about. The tourist reached him and pushed him in the chest. The young man's feet caught against the edge of the canal and his body flipped backwards as he fell. His head hit the side of the boat with a revolting crack and a moment later his body hit the water with a greasy splash. His arms and legs stirred helplessly and he sank below in a couple of seconds.

The tourist walked away from there, breathing heavily. His face and his hands were covered in cold sweat. His whole body was shaking and he bent down to throw up in his feet. Nothing could be seen or heard back from the canal.

He swallowed with difficulty and wiped his mouth with the back of his hand. It had been foolish and dangerous to follow this man all night and finally push him into the canal. But it would have been even more dangerous to let him escape again, only to find him in the next city. With some luck, this spot could be out of range of the nearest security camera. All the same, the tourist felt more unclean than he had ever felt in his life.

He slowly walked away from the canal. His knees were shaking and sometimes he had to lean against the walls to rest for a while, but in this he was not so different than most other people walking along the street at this hour. He was thinking that if this fool had succeeded in following the trail of information he was leaving behind, he was obviously not covering his tracks as well as he told himself. He was thinking that after he had committed murder in such a primal and base manner, he preferred not to be forced to do it again. He was thinking – and it was only this thought that gave him enough strength to walk back to his hotel, take a very hot shower and lie down with a sigh on his narrow bed to sink into a dreamless sleep – that this might turn out to be the last order that he was going to take.

After all, he was doing much better with hotel reviews.

PART TWO

13. Djerba

The killer liked Amsterdam. He had visited several times and always had a great time. The city had something of the atmosphere of an old pirate port where laws were different. He liked the fact that he was able to buy anything, no questions asked; he felt in his element in the chaos of different cultures – European, African, Asian – bustling along the stern façades of the canal houses; he adored Dutch women – tall and pale and blonde.

The killer was also tall and big but not in the least pale. The colour of his skin suggested the Mediterranean, the Balkans or the Levant. (But perhaps it suggested wrong.) He had dark, attentive eyes, but one half of his face was stiff with partial paresis, so there was no way that he could be called handsome. In spite of this, he laughed often and loudly and he exerted such self-confidence that people – especially women – often found him attractive. When he was travelling, he usually spoke in the local language – and somehow he managed to communicate with everyone, no matter how fantastically he abused it. And the killer travelled a lot. The interests of the people that he worked for reached across the globe.

He checked in a cheap hotel near the port (even when he had substantial amounts at his disposal, he simply did not care for such things), went out immediately and made for the red lights district. At a street corner, he found an iron box with the local newspaper to pick up. On page one was the news that police presence in the district was to remain increased after the accident with some tourist who had fallen into the canal in a state of inebriation, had hit his head against a boat and had subsequently drowned. The killer grunted and threw the newspaper on the street without slowing down.

He had to meet the owner of the hotel who had contacted him in the afternoon and he killed the time until the meeting by smoking some hashish in one of the notorious coffee shops by the canals. The drug was less potent than the Middle Eastern variety that he was accustomed to. Then he walked to the hotel which was situated above an Arab diner on the main street leading from the railway station to the centre of the city, arrived fifteen minutes late because he had to devour a kebab, and asked for the Russian. The girl at the reception – nothing special – radiated awe when she brought him into a hotel room on the first floor that the owner clearly used for his office. They were not alone. The Russian was one of those bosses who cannot exist without the presence of security. There was a huge thug wearing a tracksuit in the room with him. The boss was also wearing a tracksuit.

The killer sat opposite the hotel owner and smiled encouragingly with one half of his face. The boss did not react but the thug grimaced. They spoke in Russian.

The boss turned an open laptop to face him and the killer leaned in towards the screen. It was some kind of tourist website. There was a photograph of the hotel that they were in, the address and a phone number. Instead of the usual dozen or so sentences about the hotel, there was a long list of other hotels under the photograph and they were all clearly better. The killer shook his head in amusement and remarked that this advertisement was pointless.

The Russian slammed the laptop shut as if he wanted to break it. Then he motioned with his hand impatiently, without turning around, the thug stirred to life and brought out a frozen bottle of vodka and two glasses from the minibar. The boss opened the bottle, filled the glasses and raised one. The killer also raised his glass, they took a deep breath and drank them off in one go.

He was right, such advertisement was pointless. The cursed little man who had signed the review on the tourist website had checked into the hotel without calling anybody, stayed for a single night and left. And a few days later, this was published on the internet. The hotel owner took it as an insult. If the stupid journalist had behaved properly, the boss would have personally made sure that he was given the best room and none of his wishes were refused. If he had introduced himself, the boss did not even think it unlikely that the journalist would have found under his pillow an envelope stuffed with banknotes to be further motivated to write better things. Instead, the son of a bitch had written this.

He filled their glasses again and they drank them off in one go. The hotel owner suddenly seemed to remember that there was someone else in the room with them, waved the thug to come closer and filled a glass for him, too. The three of them drank together and the hotel boss warmly grabbed his thug by the neck and shook him. His eyes were glistening when he turned towards the killer and asked him if he thought that the behaviour of the journalist rat had been proper manly behaviour. The killer sadly shook his head. Of course not. It was perfectly clear what had to be done with him.

That is right, it was perfectly clear what had to be done with him, the Russian confirmed sternly and filled the glasses again. They drank them off in one go, then his ruddy face was lit by a wide smile and he announced that it was enough business talk for one night and now they were going to have fun. The killer did not mind. He liked fun. This was exactly why he had chosen this profession.

The boss called reception to have another bottle of vodka brought up to the room, then he gave detailed instructions to the girl what to order from the restaurant when she brought the vodka. The killer followed her with his eyes as she was leaving the room, the Russian noticed it and shook his finger in mock warning, then he burst out in a thunderous laughter, joined by the killer and the thug, made a show out of taking out his gold mobile phone and murmured something in it. Then he cut the connection, they had another glass in one go, he seemed to change his mind and made another call, even more discreetly.

The girls arrived first. There were two of them, tall and thin like fillies, with almost identical colourless faces, blue eyes and long blonde hair – one had hers in a ponytail and the other in a plait. They introduced themselves with Russian names but they said little else, although they displayed obvious experience when they joined in the drinking of vodka and, later, in the snorting of the cocaine that was brought to the room. At some point in the evening, the food from the restaurant was brought up as well, but by then the entertainment had taken a different direction: the girls were sitting on both sides of the killer, leaning on his shoulders and touching his knees, while the boss had lit a stinking cigar and seemed to be lost in the thick clouds of smoke, emitting occasional phrases in Russian. The plates with the cold dinner were sitting in the middle of the table, among the empty bottles, the full ashtrays and the disconnected lines of white powder, until the boss took his thug by the neck again in a demonstration of the warmest friendship and ordered him to start with the dinner since no one else wanted to eat. The thug, who had managed to get equally drunk in the meantime, pulled back in a hurt way and pouted which made all of them, the hotel boss, the killer and the girls, burst out laughing. Then something occurred that no one had seen coming: one moment, the thug was sitting with his face very red and staring straight at the killer looking like he was about to leap on him and tear him to pieces; the next moment, a fork was already sticking out of his ear, blood was gushing everywhere and the killer had leaned back between the two girls.

There was a moment of confusion, then the thug started to roar and bellow with pain and the prostitutes screamed for a short while but then they stopped. The boss looked first at his bodyguard and then at the killer and stayed motionless for a while, with his mouth open and his hand midway to it, holding yet another glass of vodka and the smoking cigar. Then he suddenly started laughing, the killer laughed as well, the girls relaxed and the boss brought out his mobile phone again to call someone and have them take his thug to the hospital.

After order was restored and the party could continue, the hotel boss fell asleep sitting in his armchair. The killer finished the vodka, pulled the girls' heads off the table where they were sniffing around for the last remains of the cocaine, took them to the bed, roughly took their clothes off and had sex first with one and then with the other before he finally made them kneel before him while he stood above them and came on their upturned faces.

Then he found a pen, scribbled down a few numbers on the hand of the sleeping boss, patted his cheek, put his clothes back on and went back to his hotel to sleep.

The killer did not like flying. It was not that he was afraid of flying – he just did not like to travel in anything that he did not drive himself. Perhaps one day he would buy a small private jet to use for work. He smiled. Perhaps he could paint the side with the motto "Death From Above".

His target – the journalist whom the sensitive hotel owner in Amsterdam wanted erased from the face of the earth – was in Djerba. As usual, the killer demanded a price for his services which allowed him to travel without worrying for expenses. After he woke up at noon and read the text message with the location of the target (the Russian had surely paid for him to be tracked by his credit cards or his passport), the killer took a taxi to the airport and talked to the considerably sexy young woman at the information desk until she drew up his flight plan: the shortest route went through Rome and Tunis and a domestic flight to the seaside resort of Djerba. Seaside resort sounded pretty good. The young woman from the information desk seemed ready to leave it all behind and fly away with him.

After the eventful night at the hotel of the Russian boss, the killer slept through most of the flight that he checked in for using one of his fake passports. He was waking up only when they were serving food, obliterating it and going back to sleep. Nevertheless, when he landed in Djerba at noon on the following day, he was hungry again.

The killer loved this part of the world. He had grown up among Muslims and he felt at home anyplace where they were mainly men in slippers on the street and women were few and hid their faces; where his rough voice, brusque manners and distorted face made people take a step back from him when he walked by, but then they turned to look at him in awe and respect; where life's pleasures – coffee strong as poison, tobacco, sweets, bargaining over every single thing – were not sunk and forgotten beneath all kinds of concerns and directives and a Western sense of guilt.

An exceptionally dilapidated taxi which seemed to be rolling on the wave of deafening Oriental music blasting out of its speakers deposited him in front of the fish market in the maze of commercial alleys which served as the centre of the city. He knew such places and he made his way through the crowd with confidence, waving off the offers of the vendors on both sides. He stopped for a minute on front of the stall where a dignified master fisherman with a white apron and a flower behind his ear was holding the auction for freshly caught fish, held high above his head by two younger assistants, then he found the almost invisible side alley which led to a tiny restaurant with two plastic tables. One of them was occupied by a very old man dressed in a black woollen suit despite the heat, who slowly and methodically worked every bite in his toothless mouth, staring straight ahead, before he swallowed it. Dozens of flies were circling him, landing on his fish, but he paid them no attention. The killer respectfully greeted him and sat down on the next table where he ate a lot of grilled fish caught only this morning outside of Djerba. At the end, he burped loudly to demonstrate his satisfaction for the benefit of the restaurant owner who was grilling the fish behind the stall, wiped his fingers on his trousers and took out the cheap mobile phone that he was going to throw away before leaving the country to check the name of the hotel where his target was staying.

The hotel was outside the city limits, built in the style of the stone dwellings with round doors and windows which were typical of Tunisia. There were paths between the villas, deep in flowers and green leaves, and palms were swaying in the breeze above the rooftops. On the way from the reception area to his villa, the hotel employee told him that the owner's express wish was that not a single building in the hotel was to be higher than a palm tree, and the buildings were situated among the growing trees in such a way as to avoid cutting any of them down. The killer tipped him generously, threw his stuff on the bed, put on his swimming trunks and walked barefoot down to the pool.

He did not need a photograph to recognise the man that he had to kill. In the late afternoon by the pool, the man was the only hotel guest who was not in a swimsuit. He was wearing cotton trousers, a shirt, summer shoes and socks; he was sitting at the bar and carefully sipping a very tall transparent cocktail. He was alone and his eyes never stopped darting about while his face was frozen in a friendly mask, as if he was ready to smile any moment if someone talked to him, but no one talked to him except the bartender. Every once in a while, he opened a black notebook and wrote down something in it, then he closed it and carefully put the elastic band back on the cover. He was older than the young families with children having fun around the pool and much younger than the pensioners patiently sunning themselves in the back rows of lounging chairs.

The killer walked by him and smelled a good men's perfume, laced with a slight stink of sweat. He wrinkled his nose and, never slowing down, leaped in the pool. He swam a few noisy lengths, then he noticed two young women sitting alone in lounging chairs at the edge of the water, armed with cocktails and thick magazines, smiled to himself, dove deeper and broke the surface right next to them, shaking water out of his hair. The girls looked up from their magazines. The one who was sitting near was ginger and plump and the other one had black hair and a slim, elongated body. He squatted down next to the one who was sitting near.

The conversation lasted several minutes. The sarcasm of the black-haired girl broke against the impenetrable indifference of the killer who was supremely uninterested in her opinion of him, so she finally gave a last warning stare to her friend and retreated into the sanctuary of her magazine. The ginger-haired one had already closed hers and was laughing at his clumsy attempts to imitate her Australian accent. He offered to get them both a drink from the bar. Not looking up from her magazine, the black-haired one remarked that the hotel was all-inclusive which somewhat devaluated his generosity. He asked the ginger-haired one what she wanted. She coquettishly replied that she would not mind another drink but she needed to get her hat from the room because the sun was beginning to hurt her. He replied with understanding that women with such ginger hair and such lovely freckles should protect their looks even more carefully than the rest. When he said "lovely freckles", he ran his fingertips lightly on her upper arm, like he was touching a musical instrument. The girl giggled, left her magazine and asked her friend if she wanted anything from the room. The black-haired one icily replied that she did not want anything. He stood up before the ginger-haired one and offered her his hand to help her stand up from the lounging chair, then he offered to keep her company to the room and back. The girl's eyes darted in the direction of her friend, but the black-haired one did not say anything, sharply turning the next page of her magazine instead.

The killer followed the ginger-haired girl down the alleys of rose bushes and bees buzzing among them, entered their room after her, caught her by the waist and tossed her on the bed. Her eyes and her mouth remained wide open when he pulled off her bikini panties and when he entered her; she was already so wet that he went all the way in with the first thrust.

Several hours later, after he had had a shower in his room, the killer entered the hotel restaurant, heaped a tremendous amount of food on several plates and ate his dinner alone at a corner table. From his spot, he could see the target who was also eating alone, in the opposite corner. The two of them were the only men in the restaurant sitting by themselves. There was also an older lady with pearls who was sitting alone, graciously accepting the attention of the waiters and sipping her glass of white wine.

The target was having white wine as well, but unlike the older lady, he already had two empty bottles on his table. He had opened his laptop and was pecking away on the keyboard, deep in concentration, drinking wine and sometimes smiling to himself or to something that he saw on the screen. The two Australian girls were not in the restaurant. The black-haired one probably did not eat dinner to keep in shape; the ginger-haired one was probably not able to get up from the bed.

The killer stood up, walked across the restaurant, pulled a chair for himself and sat down next to the man with the laptop. He looked up from the screen, surprised, and his forehead wrinkled like he was trying to remember if they had met. The killer smiled as affably as he could and asked him what was so interesting in this computer. The man gave him another look, then he shrugged and turned his laptop so that he could see the screen. Then he explained that he was an author of hotel reviews for a tourist website and he had just completed the review for the hotel that they were staying in. The killer said that this was very interesting. The man clearly needed to tell someone about his job, because he immediately offered to show him the new review. The killer readily agreed. The man reached and proudly hit a key. On the screen, there was a sequence of amateur photographs of the hotel – showing the pool, the villas, the reception building, the palms and so on – accompanied by the theme music of a famous animated series about two families from the stone age. Every two photographs of the hotel alternated with a frame from the animated series. The similarity between the architectural style and interior design of the hotel and the animated depiction of the Stone Age was indeed remarkable. The man started to giggle. The short film ended. The killer asked him if the hotel owner would not be offended when he opened the tourist website and saw this instead of the review that he had been expecting. The man gave him a long look, then he shook his head and turned the laptop back towards himself. He pretended to be finishing something, then he wished him a pleasant night without looking up from the screen. The killer stood up, patted his shoulder amiably (the man involuntarily cringed) and walked away.

He was going to kill him tonight. He only had to wait until the man went back to his room and fell asleep, then he would choke him with his own pillow. Nothing personal, just business.

There was an amphitheatre in the hotel complex, offering evening entertainment. Tonight was traditional Tunisian music and there were several grim-looking men with moustaches on the stage, pulling on the strings of their instruments, while a big lady with a shimmering green long-sleeved dress that covered almost every centimetre of her body was murmuring something filled with melancholy under her breath. The killer turned around to leave but then he noticed the black-haired friend of the ginger-haired Australian who was sitting alone on one of the back rows of the amphitheatre, sipping her cocktail.

When he sat down next to her, she started but then she recognised him and relaxed a little. Then she sipped from her cocktail again and told him that her friend was feeling tired and she was going to stay in their room for the night. He did not say anything. He was sitting with the better half of his face to her and his lips twitched in a smile. The black-haired Australian started telling him something but she was slurring a little and her accent was stronger than before so the man was not quite sure what she was saying. Most often of all, he discerned the words "she" and "I", but the overall intonation told him that the young woman was not very pleased with the situation and with her life in general.

He listened for several minutes, then he turned to her, casually caught her by the neck and pressed her lips to his. The girl froze and tried to pull back her head, but he was holding her firmly. Several seconds passed, then she opened her mouth and let him inside it. The kiss did not last for long. The girl pulled herself out of his arms and told him that this was not the most appropriate place to behave in this way. He looked around. Not much could be seen in the semi-darkness of the amphitheatre, but he offered her to take a walk with him in the garden all the same. The girl agreed.

They took a walk in the garden. When they were far enough from the path, he pushed her against the trunk of a palm, lifted up her dress, pulled down her panties, turned her with her back to him, pressed her face against the tree and fucked her long and hard, keeping his hand on her mouth to silence her moaning.

Then he walked to the villa where the target was staying. The villa was at the end of a path, in the shadow of some tall rose bushes. The killer smiled crookedly in the dark. As usual, fortune favoured the wicked.

He squatted by the door and pulled out the key card for his own room, but instead of swiping it through the lock, he used it to ease the latch. The door opened with an almost inaudible click, he pushed it open with his fingertips and crawled into the room without standing up. His eyes had already adjusted to the darkness so it only took him several seconds to figure out where he was. Even before that, his nose had already told him that something was not right. The room of the man smelled like a hotel – cleaning agents, new furniture and bathroom cosmetics – but there was no human smell. The killer slowly stood up with his back to the wall. The bed was empty and made. There were no objects in the room except for the same ones that the killer had seen in his own room. There were no clothes in the open wardrobe. He reached behind himself and switched the lights on. There was no one in the room.

The killer walked out of the room, closed the door behind him and went to the hotel reception. The night shift was a woman who looked about thirty-five years old, with dreadlocks and tattoos swirling under the short sleeves of her uniform shirt. He asked her about the guest in the room that he was coming from; she smiled and explained that the man had just left. In the middle of the night? Obviously, he had to take a late flight out of Djerba airport – guests of the resort often had to do that if there was no direct flight from Djerba to wherever they were going and they had to arrive in time for the morning flights out of the larger international airport in Tunis. He let out a curse in his native language under his breath, but he pulled himself together, smiled and thanked for the information. The receptionist leaned in to him and asked him if it had been something important, with genuine concern. The killer replied that they were old friends and they had not seen each other in years, and now they had stayed in the same hotel in Djerba by chance – but then his friend had left without even saying goodbye. It seemed that fate had decided to keep them apart after all. The woman smiled and looked up at him, and then she suggested that fate knew what it was doing. He asked her what she meant. The woman replied that her shift was ending in two hours and if he was still up, she was going to show him this hotel's best kept secret.

Two hours later the killer was waiting for her in front of the reception building with a bottle of rum that he had gotten absolutely free from the restaurant kitchen. (The door was not even locked.) The hotel's best kept secret turned out to be a tiny cove, accessible only by a narrow path between the bushes. The lights of the resort coloured the sky behind them in bluish yellow, but above the sea, only the silver crescent of the moon could be seen. The water was not as warm as he expected, but after they shared the bottle of rum, they took their clothes off (neither of them had a swimsuit on), walked into the sea grunting and puffing and started swimming in. In the moonlight, with her hair spilling around her and her wiry body, the woman seemed like a beautiful predator to him, an animal that he had to tame. He swam back towards the shore and when he reached the shallows, turned on his back and floated with his arms and legs apart. In a few minutes, the woman returned and pressed herself against him, her skin cool to the touch. He was ready for her and their bodies locked, rolling and turning in the waves. When he felt that he was about to come, he dug his feet in the cold sand on the bottom, reached with his arms and locked his fingers in her thick hair, then he pushed her head down, under the water surface, still thrusting with his hips. Surprised, the woman tried to twist out of his grip. He tensed his muscles and pushed her head down into the sand. Just a little more. The woman was struggling more wildly now. He growled and his whole body shook in a last powerful thrust. Then he let go and released her head from his grip. The woman swam up with chaotic movements, her eyes open very wide, breathing in furiously, then she found him in the dark water and tried to hit him but the killer caught her wrist and clenched her so hard that she twisted in pain. Their eyes met. His gaze was calm and heavy. The woman hissed, tore out of his grip and waded back to the beach.

He turned on his back, spread his arms and legs and gazed at the night sky. The waves were rocking him like a cradle. The killer lazily wondered whether he was going to drown if he fell asleep in the sea. He decided that he was not – nature took care of its own.

14. Malta

The tourist often had nightmares in which he had lost his way. In his dream he knew that he was in a particular city, but when he looked up from the map in his hands, from his watch or the display of his mobile phone, the familiar city looked completely different, even though it was undoubtedly the same. Deprived of anything that could point him in the right direction, he started roaming the streets and having meaningless conversations with the people passing by in a language that he knew and he did not know at the same time, until finally he woke up, panting, his heart beating wildly, to switch on the lamp on the nightstand, look around the hotel room that he found himself in, switch off the lamp and try to go back to sleep.

In Malta, it was more or less the same in real life. He had a guidebook with a city map, but the Maltese names of the streets were so confusing – in a Semitic language which used the Latin alphabet – that his memory refused to connect them with something familiar and every time he looked up from the map in his hands to the street sign, he had already forgotten what he had just read. The whole island confused him – it was like they had taken a piece of the Arab world and towed it somewhere near the Italian coast, by way of the British Empire.

Sleep deprivation made it worse. He had to take a late flight out of Djerba airport in Tunisia and, of course, there was no immediate connection to Malta until the next morning. The airport people offered him a minibus transfer to the city where he could stay in a hotel, but when they calculated the time in which he had to be back at the airport to check in for the morning flight to Malta, it left him less than four hours at the hotel, so the tourist refused. Instead, he walked around the empty halls of the airport and finally settled in an unpleasant, poorly lit restaurant where he was hoping he could get a drink and watch some sport on the television, but instead he was forced to eat a five-course midnight dinner offered by the airline and watch some television show in Arabic with French subtitles which probably would not have made sense even if it had been in his native language.

The hotel in Valetta that he had to review was located on the promenade, with a view to the fort, and when he entered the lobby, it seemed vaguely familiar, even though it was his first time in Malta. The receptionist was clearly used to meeting guests who stopped at the door and started looking around, trying to remember where they had seen this place, because he approached him with a smile, offered his hand and told him the title of the film which had been shot here. The film was quite popular, directed by one of the world's most acclaimed film directors, and it featured the star of the secret agent films before he had become so popular. The Valetta hotel had been used as a stand-in for another hotel, somewhere in the Middle East, which had been the base of a hit squad of Israeli intelligence tasked with eliminating some terrorists. Of course, one could buy the film at the reception. The tourist was ready to decline by force of habit (he had never come upon something really valuable that could be purchased at a hotel reception), but then he had an idea how to use the film for his hotel review and bought the disc.

His room was comfortably featureless. The tourist took out his laptop, considered the power outlet on the wall, went down to reception, borrowed an adapter (the receptionist had already prepared it for him), went back up, switched on his laptop and could not resist the temptation to open his profile on the other website, but no one needed assistance to commit suicide in Malta anyway. He sighed with relief, closed it, put on the disc with the film and noted down the minutes and seconds in which one could see the façade, lobby and rooms of the hotel in the background. Then he yawned, opened a beer from the minibar and walked out on the tiny balcony. It looked on the bay which was clearly hosting some kind of speedboat race. The tourist brought out a chair.

In the afternoon, he took a walk. He even took a few photographs that he was not planning to use for his review, just for the pleasure of it. Then he bought a bottle of local beer from a grocery store and went down to the edge of the old city where one could see the waves breaking, but when he sat down on a fort wall to drink it, he discovered that he had no way to open the bottle, so he had to walk back up to the store to get it open and by then he did not feel like going back down to the wall so he drank the beer on the walk back into town.

On the next morning, he woke up in surprisingly good shape (he had had just two bottles of red wine with dinner in a restaurant in the cellar of some medieval fortress) and he read the guidebook while he was having coffee on the balcony. He decided to take a boat to Gozo – the neighbouring, smaller island, where he could see the famous blue lagoon which had been the location for several popular films. In this way, he could leave Malta on the following day, feeling certain that he had acquainted himself with the most important things that the island had to offer.

When he arrived at the port, the tourist boat to Gozo had already left and the next one departed in the late afternoon. The tourist looked helplessly around and sat down on a bench where he was immediately besieged by several impudent sea birds. He stood up; forcing the birds to fly away with querulous cries, went back to the ticket booth and asked if this was the only way to reach the island. The woman behind the counter smoothed down her moustache, deep in thought, produced an ancient mobile phone out of her pocket and made a show of dialling a number, and then she had a noisy conversation with someone on the other side. Finally, she cut the connection and informed him that a private captain of a motorboat was about to come and pick him up to transport him to Gozo. Of course, the price was higher, but the terms were better – the guy with the motorboat would take him there and back when he wanted to.

The motorboat captain was a sly old man with a bright red sleeveless shirt and mirrored sunglasses who kept talking in such an exotic form of English that the tourist did not understand a word. The motorboat was equipped with a sound system which pumped out techno music. When they left the port, the captain offered him to drive the motorboat for a while if he wanted to, but the tourist did not want to. Instead, he was sitting at the stern, clutching the metal railing, certain that he was about to fly out of the motorboat any moment as it bucked and leaped over the waves.

The blue lagoon was a disappointingly tiny bay on a tiny island – Gozo could only be seen as a yellow smudge on the horizon and Malta could not be seen at all. There was a small quay and a smaller beach but both were crammed with tourists. Motorboats and yachts kept coming to the quay and unloading new ones. The tourist arranged with the captain to come and pick him up in an hour and disembarked. There was nothing to do. At the end of the quay was a stall selling beer and ice cream and the blue water in the lagoon was so terrifyingly cold that when he attempted to go in, his teeth started to chatter after several seconds. The tourist resigned himself to going out on the beach, sitting on the hotel towel that he had brought and waiting for the sun to restore the circulation in his legs. When the captain returned, the tourist told him that he did not want to go to Gozo at all and asked to be returned to the port in Malta from which they had left.

A few hours later, he was sitting on the balcony of his room in the hotel, drinking beer. The return trip was a nightmare – he was sick just a minute after they had left. He was finally feeling better now, but he would probably not have the energy to go out for dinner. He finished the review for the hotel which had been a stand-in in the film about the

Israeli hit squad and sent it off, using the old-fashioned cable internet in his room. Then he checked the results on his previous review – the funny collage which compared the hotel in Djerba to the animated series about the Stone Age. It was only two days old but the trend was for it to become the most visited and highly ranked review that he had ever written. The tourist smiled. People would always rather ridicule something than admire it.

He carefully considered the options for reviewing hotels around the Mediterranean. After today's adventure on the motorboat, he preferred to arrive in the next place by direct flight. Most hotels in traditional French, Spanish and Italian resorts had already been reviewed before the summer season, but he managed to find an interesting one in Cairo. He had never been to Cairo. The tourist shrugged and reserved a room in the hotel, then he started searching for a flight. This time, he did not even feel like opening the other website.

He was a little bored but the problem was not so serious that it could not be fixed by a thick book and two bottles of wine in the evening when it was starting to get unbearable. The climate suited him well. He did not want to rush to a final conclusion yet, but every day the thought that all he was about to do from now on was to visit hotels and write about them, grew stronger and stronger. It had been several weeks since he had seen a dead or dying human being and he was not particularly surprised to find that he did not miss it at all.

15. Cairo

The tourist hoped that he would never have to set foot in Cairo again. Every time that he had come to a country in this part of the world, he had been on an organised transfer from the airport to the hotel and back, so that he had seen nothing else except palm trees, sea, sand and dark men with moustaches who were preparing him cocktails by the pool. When he arrived in Cairo, a bus of the travel agency working with the hotel was already waiting at the airport to take him – together with several dozens of other guests who had arrived on the same flight – on a detailed tour of the city even before they were taken to the hotel.

Cairo was the most gigantic and the dirtiest city that the tourist had ever seen. As the guide explained to them (for some unfathomable reason, in shockingly bad Russian), they had had the luck to arrive at the same time in which the capital of Egypt (along with the whole of the Middle East) was celebrating one of the most important Muslim holidays, so that no one was working and the entire population spent the whole day on the street. The traffic jams were ridiculous. The city highways were clogged with squatting pedestrians and shitting donkeys who forced all cars to grind to a halt and use their horns liberally in an attempt to budge them. The endless neighbourhoods on both sides of the highway seemed to consist entirely of half-ruined blocks of flats with missing walls and roofs and lines for washing stretching from one to the next. The city looked like it had been bombed for years, but, in fact, it was the years that had bombed it.

Every time the bus stopped to unload them at some tourist attraction, silent men with uniforms and machine guns stood guard at the front and the back of the bus while the tourists were getting on and off. The guide nonchalantly explained that tourist buses were a favourite target of terrorists who used car-bombs. Every time they got off the bus, they were swarmed by dozens of males ranging from five to fifty-five years old, all trying to sell them something.

Even the air in Cairo seemed crowded – as if too many people had breathed it for too long. In addition to breathing, many of them had driven cars and trucks with diesel engines, eaten spiced food, broken wind and raised domestic animals and beasts of burden who had also broken wind.

They visited a museum of papyrus, a museum of perfume and a museum of cotton. All three museums were more like shops selling respectively papyri with the names of the tourists spelled with Egyptian hieroglyphs, dizzyingly heavy perfumes in small glass vials, and cotton kerchiefs with the names of the tourists spelled with Egyptian hieroglyphs.

After this, they visited the Pyramids. The Pyramids were gigantic and dirty as well. When they disembarked from the bus, they were crowded by Bedouins with dirty white turbans who offered the tourists to ride their camels. Some of the tourists agreed to ride the camels. The camels immediately proceeded to ride off in a gallop in an arbitrary direction. The tourists happily screamed that they wanted to get off. The Bedouins got up on other camels, rode after them and asked for money to make the camels of the tourists stop and kneel down so that they could get off. The tourist did not ride a camel but could not avoid a wrinkled old man who looked the same age as the stone monuments around and put in his hand a small stone with an Egyptian hieroglyph on it, insisting that it was a special present for the tourist and then insisting to get some money for it before he left. After they had looked at some Pyramids, they got back on the bus and were finally taken to their hotel.

The hotel was shocking. It was located in a ramshackle building next to a six-lane city highway with a myriad cars, people and animals crawling along in a state of perpetual traffic jam. It was neither in Cairo's historical centre nor in Giza but somewhere in the neighbourhoods in between the two. There was a gas station on one side of the hotel and a half-ruined block of flats on the other side. The door of his room opened with an old metal key and did not close properly. The window did not open at all. The room looked straight on the highway and, by some paradox of physics, the noise of the cars crawling outside was not muffled but amplified until it became deafening. "The view to the Pyramids" which the guide described with abandon while they were on the bus boiled down to the fact that if the tourist stood on his toes in a particular way right next to the window, he could just glimpse the top of a Pyramid between the high-rises at the end of the highway. The water coming out of the bathroom faucets was yellow-brownish in colour and the plumbing was making a plaintive, howling noise. The bathroom itself looked like someone had committed suicide in it and the cleaning lady had run off screaming for the police instead of doing her job.

The tourist stood in the middle of the room. The owners of this hotel had contacted the tourist website to ask for a review and this had brought him here. Did they really think that after he had seen their hotel, he would be inspired to write a masterpiece? He would have done much better if he had never come to the hotel at all. Unless... he opened his laptop and quickly typed in a few sentences. It was working. The idea was to describe the hotel meticulously, by the usual criteria – location, architecture, furnishing – using only negative adjectives. He opened a synonym finder in a separate window to facilitate the task. He was working with gusto. It was late in the afternoon and the traffic on the highway outside was intensifying, along with the noise.

The door of his room was kicked open. The room was not large and the man who burst in with a gun in his hand seemed to fill it at once. The tourist froze with his fingers over the keyboard of his laptop and his mouth hanging open. The man with the gun reached behind with his free hand and closed the door. The gun was big and black and the muzzle looked ludicrously long because of the silencer. The man had several days' worth of thick stubble and shiny curly hair. He looked local but he spoke English with an indeterminate accent.

The first thing that he said was the name of the hotel in Amsterdam that the tourist had stayed in recently. When the man opened his mouth to speak, the tourist noticed that one half of his face was paralysed and only then remembered that he had already seen him – in the hotel in Djerba where he had gone from Amsterdam. The man had sat down at his table and the tourist had shown him the review with the frames from the animated series that he had completed a few hours before he had left on the night flight to Tunis.

The man kept the gun pointed at his face while he explained to him why he had come. The owner of the Amsterdam hotel had taken his review as a personal insult and a threat to his business that called for the tourist to be punished. The man was a killer for hire. The tourist listened to him with irrational calm. His body was still not able to react to everything that was happening. In the killer's personal view, the order to eliminate him was an overreaction on part of the hotel owner, but... he shrugged. Nothing personal, just business.

The tourist hated people who used this phrase. He finally stirred and reached with his hand to close his laptop. The killer calmly ordered him to put his hands on the laptop so that he could see them. The tourist obeyed.

The killer continued to tell him how he had gotten to him. After he had missed him in Djerba, he had called the hotel owner. The hotel owner had been irritated by the idea of spending more money (he had to pay someone to track the tourist by his next hotel reservation and then pay transport expenses to the killer so that he could get there as well), so they had had a short argument about the price and the killer had finally agreed to do it for free. The killer asked him if he wanted to know why he was ready to kill him for free. The tourist shook his head stiffly. The killer pulled a chair and sat on it backwards, resting his gun arm on the backseat. The gun was no longer pointing straight towards the face of the tourist but the killer would need just a fraction of a second to point it again.

After he had arrived in Cairo, he had gone to see the Pyramids. He always saw the sights; otherwise his job would have been too monotonous. Some natives (the killer used another word which was more offensive and completely incorrect from an ethnical point of view) had offered him a camel to ride and he had said yes, why not. And then – the killer started laughing as he was telling this – the damn animal had taken off to somewhere. The dirty natives had followed him on other camels and had asked him for money to make his camel stop so that he could get off. He had chosen another option. He had jumped off the camel while it was still on the run, and then he had grabbed the nearest camel rider's leg while he was going by, he had pulled him off his camel and he had beaten the shit out of him. Instead of helping their friend, the other camel riders had taken off in a gallop. While he was beating the guy with the camel, two cops had shown up – on camels as well. They talked for a while and convinced him that they were on his side in this matter. Then the policemen invited him to the shack where they were resting in the shade and offered him tea. Half an hour later, after he had gained their trust and parted with a certain amount of cash, the killer already had this gun at his disposal.

He reached into a trouser pocket with his free hand and showed the tourist a cheap mobile phone. While he had been negotiating with the cops, the hotel owner in Amsterdam had tracked down the tourist and had sent the killer a text message with the name of his Cairo hotel. After his job was completed, the killer would confirm it on this same phone and then throw it in the first garbage can and finally have a well-deserved rest. It was his first time chasing a man on two continents. Was it two continents? The tourist nodded stiffly.

The killer put the mobile phone back in his pocket, raised his other arm and pulled the trigger from a metre away.

There was a dry click. The tourist blinked. Nothing else happened.

He emitted an inchoate sound, grabbed his closed laptop that his hands were lying on, and swung with it sideways. It was more by chance that he managed to hit the killer in the face with the edge of the computer. He tried to hit him again, but the man had excellent reflexes and he was already leaping back on his feet and pushing his chair forward, so the tourist missed his face. It was by pure chance that something better happened – he hit him in the gun arm and hit him so hard that the killer dropped his gun and the tourist dropped his laptop.

This was his last small victory. He still had not managed to get up from his own chair when the killer fell on him and knocked him to the ground, then he easily brushed aside the tourist's hands with which he was trying to protect himself and landed five or six not particularly powerful but jarring blows in the bottom half of the tourist's face, enough to stun him. Then the killer twisted to the side without getting up off the tourist, grabbed his gun and tried to point it at his face again, but the silenced muzzle was so long that the killer was forced to take up an uncomfortable position with his hands close to his chest.

The tourist did the only thing that he could do in this moment: he grabbed the muzzle of the gun and put all his strength in trying to twist it up and away from his own face. This turned out to be not as difficult as he had expected – again because of the long muzzle that gave him the advantage of the lever. The killer gave out a short, business-like grunt, changed his grip on the weapon and pulled it out of the tourist's hands, managing to land an elbow in his face in the meantime.

The tourist, who had not stopped trying to grab something around himself with his free hand, finally felt the familiar shape of his laptop with his fingertips, caught it and swung it once again at the killer's head as he was leaning over him. This time, he managed to land the corner of the laptop's body somewhere in the vicinity of the killer's temple and he hit him so hard that the laptop broke apart in his hand and the two halves flew off in different directions. The killer groaned and slumped to the side but the room was so narrow that his body rested against the wall.

The tourist squeaked and started trying to crawl out from beneath the killer's heavy body sitting on his chest. It was not easy to do. It took him so long that the killer started to come back around, shaking his head and blinking furiously.

At this moment, the tourist had managed to slip halfway out, so he sat on the floor, grabbed with his two hands the hand of the killer which was holding the gun and started to twist it. He would have never made it if the other man had been conscious, as he was much heavier and stronger, but the tourist succeeded to beat him to it, pulled the weapon out of his grip, clumsily rotated it to point at the face of the killer and pressed the trigger with his thumb – the only way that he could do it from this awkward position.

This time, the suspect gun that the killer had procured from the corrupt representatives of Egyptian law enforcement decided to give it a shot. There was a muffled explosion, followed by something like a piercing hiss, and the gun leaped back from the recoil, painfully ripping itself out of the tourist's fingers and slamming against his gut with such force that it took all air out of him.

The other end of the weapon still managed to inflict greater damage. Shot almost point-blank, the bullet ripped the killer's neck somewhere under his chin, pierced his lower jaw, came back out through his cheek, grazed his ear and finally buried itself somewhere in the ceiling. The man roared with pain and clutched the wound with his hand but bright red blood started immediately spurting out from between his fingers. The large artery leading to the brain had been severed.

The tourist continued to twist his body in panic, trying to get out. The man reached with his other hand, more by reflex than really trying to get a hold on him, but his strength was leaving him with every beat of his heart pumping blood out of the wound.

The tourist finally managed to struggle free but he could not keep his balance, staggered backwards and fell on the floor once again. He crawled back, grabbing fistfuls of the carpet and kicking out, until his back hit the wall. He kept staring at the man who kept looking at him as well. The man's eyes grew dim. His mouth remained half-open. Finally, the man died.

The tourist must have breathed in the meantime but he could not remember doing it. Now he took in breath with such force that he started coughing. He expected the noise of the struggle to attract someone's attention, but it must have been so loud in the hotel that no one had noticed the additional banging coming from his room.

He gathered his strength and stood up, carefully leaned over the killer who remained on his knees, resting against the wall, with his head hanging on his chest, and picked up the gun. He went to the bathroom, put the weapon in the sink and spent several seconds trying to decide what he needed to do more, vomit or relieve himself out of the opposite end. Then he cleaned himself as well as he could, rinsed the gun, held it in toilet paper and brought it back to the room where he left the weapon purchased from the Egyptian police in front of the dead man. Everything was covered in blood. All that he could do was collect the remains of his laptop. He went back to the bathroom, took the plastic bag lining the trash bin and put both halves of the laptop in it before he put it back in his bag. He looked around. There was nothing else in the room that he had brought with him. He was hoping that any investigation that was about to ensue would be convoluted and hushed enough so that it would not lead to him.

The tourist held his breath, leaned over the killer and pulled the mobile phone out of his pocket. All calls and text messages were to the same unidentified number with a long international code. The last received message contained the name of this hotel. The tourist replied to it with the text "Order completed", then he thought some more and added: "Nothing personal, just business".

He put the phone in his pocket. He was going to dispose of it, together with the broken laptop. He reckoned that the hotel owner in Amsterdam would be satisfied enough with this outcome. There was a certain amount of risk that he would learn of the killer's death after a while, but the tourist was hoping that the suspicion would not fall on him – after all, the hotel owner was convinced that he was nothing more than a bad review writer.

The safest strategy was probably to go back to Amsterdam and kill the hotel owner. But the tourist was simply not this kind of person. If he had a choice, he always preferred to run instead of acting on it. His experience demonstrated that the world always forgot about him.

He looked around once again, walked out of the hotel room and carefully closed the door behind himself.

16. Italy

The tourist was horrified to discover that he was not able to relax. He had always imagined that after he had retired from his second profession – he thought of it as retirement as his main income did come from the other website and not from reviewing hotels – his life would become a lazy string of small pleasures and equally small impulsive decisions. (To stay one more day in the town of X, to travel to the city of Y with the only purpose of tasting that vodka martini once again.)

Instead, it had not been two days in Como before the emptiness which filled every day from the beginning until the end started to weight down on him with such force that he took refuge in compiling endless lists of petty, meaningless tasks and crossing them out one by one: to visit all the miniature towns around Lago di Como which were serviced by the public boats and have a cocktail in each one of them; to photograph all the spots around the lake that he recognised from various Hollywood films (this turned out to be easier than it sounded – it seemed that most productions, from classical American science-fiction adventures and Italian comedies to the latest film about the secret agent that he knew in excruciating detail, had chosen one and the same especially picturesque stretch of the coast); to learn one hundred Italian words a day, and the like.

On the third day, he took the train to Milan, found a store of the American company which had produced his broken laptop and bought a new one from the same model. It had been several years since he had bought the previous one so the new version of the same model actually had a larger display, better technical characteristics and improved (or at least, during the first couple of days, more difficult to use) interface, but it was the closest to his old laptop that could be purchased at the store. He owned little but he valued what little he owned, and on the rare occasions when he had to part with something, he always restored it as quickly and as closely to the original as possible. For years he had been using the same brand of laptops, the same brand of mobile phones, the same international bank for his cards, the same brand of cosmetics and a very limited number of brands for his clothes and shoes. He often thought that in an ideal world, everything that he needed would be produced by one and the same company.

He had not chosen Como by accident. The little towns by the lake consisted mostly of holiday homes and some of them housed the most famous and expensive clinics for plastic surgery and rehabilitation in Italy. The tourist arrived in the most beautiful days of spring when the hills by the lake were bright green and the water was sky blue, and checked in a small family-owned hotel on the coast with a view to the white wooden piers of the port and the opposite coast with the slowly crawling funicular. The collision with the killer for hire had rattled him more than he wanted to admit: his stomach almost immediately rejected any kind of food that he managed to put in his mouth, he had heart palpitations all the time and slept badly even after he had anesthetised himself with industrial amounts of grappa. For several days he was tortured by paranoia, as well, afraid of being recognised and followed – either by other assassins or the police – but after he travelled to Milan and back without anything remotely similar occurring, this fear gradually receded.

On the fourth day, he opened his new laptop and relished writing a review for the small hotel that he was staying in – it was an epistolary composition in the pompous style of eighteenth-century literature, consisting of several letters exchanged by a disgraced aristocrat and his mysterious inamorata. The aristocrat was staying in the same hotel (which had indeed existed back in the eighteenth century) to nurture his body and soul after a dangerous duel which had almost resulted in his death. His mysterious lover – an heiress to one of the wealthiest families in Milan and the reason for the duel – wrote back imploring him to keep his spirits up and let the healing powers of the water and the air to draw the pain from his wounds and the poison from his heart.

On the fifth day, the tourist decided to go on a tour of Italy since he was there anyway.

On the sixth day, he was standing in front of the statue of David by Michelangelo in Florence, eating a tripe sandwich. There were about ten thousand other people in the square and even though not all of them had bought a tripe sandwich, every last one of them insisted on having their photograph taken immediately in front of the statue and more or less in the same posture. The Americans posing in front of the cameras held by their wives and girlfriends would often show something tiny between their thumb and forefinger and make a sorry face. As in other places that the tourist had been to, the Russians were gradually outnumbering the Americans.

On the seventh day, he was standing in front of the most famous stairs in Rome. There were so many people that the stairs themselves could not be seen and in every shot that he took, there were about a dozen other tourists who had no idea that they were being photographed, so their eyes were half-closed in a blink or their faces were slack like the faces of cretins.

On the eighth day, he gave up travelling south as it was getting hotter every day, and took a train back north to Venice. There was a vaporetto running from the station to the starting point of one of the tourist routes at the grand canal. The sky was blindingly blue. The yellowing peeling palazzi on both sides of the canal looked like they were going to crumble down any moment. The tourist squinted against the sun and put on his sunglasses. He planned to start the day with a real Italian espresso.

The tourist did not dare to admit it yet, but the tour seemed to be agreeing with him.

A few hours later, he was standing on the bridge which was winning the competition for Italy's most crowded tourist attraction hands down. The people who wanted to walk across the bridge, pausing at the highest point to take a photograph of themselves, preferably without any other people in the same shot, were so many that they formed a literally impassable crowd – the only way to go from one end of the bridge to the other was to stop every few seconds when the ones who had reached the top stopped to take the photograph, wait and then go one or two steps further. It was like a line in a supermarket, but even slower.

The tourist was not in a hurry to get anywhere. For the first time since the Cairo incident, he felt something like tranquillity and he was determined to enjoy it for as long as it lasted.

The couple in front of him on the bridge did not seem tranquil at all. The woman was petite and elegantly dressed, with large dark eyes and perfect miniature features, like a doll. The man was big and blond and even if he had not been wearing shorts, white trainers and a small bag on his waist, no one would have mistaken him for anything but an American. He was trying to defend himself, limply saying "baby, baby" in between every few sentences the woman said, but he had no chance at all. She was like a fury, speaking English with a Latin accent and machine gun velocity and punctuating her accusations by hitting the man with one of those disposable umbrellas that the immigrants sold to the tourists for a few euros.

The woman finished her exposition, hissed and turned back from her (already ex) boyfriend. The tourist awkwardly smiled at her. In the next moment, her face underwent a magical transformation. Her dark eyes were still burning but her locked brows relaxed, her features softened and her smile revealed small and very white teeth which could indeed be described most precisely as "pearl-like". She threw a final withering glance over her shoulder, took a step forward and deftly took the tourist's arm, asking him if he wanted to take her somewhere for aperitivo or he had some other plans for the day.

Before he was able to reply, the woman had already turned him around and was pulling him in the opposite direction among the crowd of tourists preparing their cameras in expectation of reaching the midway point of the bridge. Since he did not know what else to say, the tourist introduced himself. The woman gave him an amused look, reached with her free left hand and shook his right, all the time pulling him back across the bridge.

A colourful American expletive echoed behind them but the woman ordered him to keep walking and look ahead, and the tourist did not even think to argue with her.

17. Seville

The woman was a control freak, something which the tourist could understand completely, but her insistence was on different things. Subconsciously, he was trying to leave no trace in the places that he was passing through, leaving everything just as he had found it. Very consciously, she was trying to transform every place where she found herself – even for a few hours – to reflect her own personality. Small but noticeable souvenirs appeared in hotel rooms; furniture was moved around; the shelves in the bathroom filled up with dozens of mysterious vials and the tourist's toothbrush was fitted with an elegant blue cap that she had bought for him without him noticing. The woman liked her clothes and travelled with two enormous wheeled suitcases which the tourist had to pull and carry up and down the stairs, and both packing and unpacking them lasted for several hours. His habit of throwing away the clothes that he no longer needed literally infuriated her. The tourist tried to convince her that he was not able to feel emotionally attached to a shirt that he had bought two weeks ago and she frostily noted that this was probably a symptom of his inability to feel emotionally attached to anything at all. (And she was most probably right.) The woman did not pay so much attention to food and especially to meal times, but she had the risible propensity to feel hunger precisely in those places and hours when it was particularly difficult to find anything to eat: in a tiny Italian town strewn about the hills where locating the only grocery store amounted to a feat, or at three in the morning in their room in a guest house outside of any populated area. For the tourist, meal times were sacred because they organised his otherwise empty days, and he never got hungry during the night because it was during the night that he was sleeping.

It was exactly this last thing that was their biggest issue. The tourist would have a few drinks before dinner, eat dinner and then gradually gravitate towards the bed, so that he was usually ready to go to sleep around midnight. On the other hand, he would always wake up between seven and eight in the morning, local time, and he was not able to go back to sleep, no matter how late he had gone to bed. He had been living this way for years and he could not even imagine changing it.

The woman had been born and raised in a culture that considered night life a sacrosanct right for every citizen. She would start getting ready for going out around eight in the evening when the tourist was often starting to yawn already, she was ready for dinner between ten and eleven, and around midnight she was just beginning to have a good time. Her usual bedtime was three or four in the morning, but this did not mean that she was ready to sleep. As a consequence, she liked sleeping in and she became irritable when he could not lay on his back any longer, staring at the ceiling with bloodshot eyes, got up and started doing something in their room.

Despite all this, they had a few fine days together. She had recently gotten her degree in fashion marketing and would not make compromises with the job that she wanted but this turned out to be more and more difficult because most fashion brands were financially challenged in the shrinking European market, so she did not mind just drifting from one city to the next and having a good time. He had neither the desire nor the energy to do anything else except accompany her and have sex with her – after his latest review for the small hotel in Como which had not been received very well, he was suffering from something like writer's block and he did not even open the tourist website to check if there was a suitable hotel to review along their route.

In Turin, they walked along the main shopping street which the guidebooks described as the longest pedestrian street in Europe (the tourist had visited at least half a dozen streets in various countries which laid the same claim). The street was nothing special but it was built in such a way that it opened a view to the mountains which seemed to rise immediately where the city ended. Even now, in summer, when Italian women were wearing provocative flower dresses with almost invisible underwear and Italian men were sweating in their suits with narrow ties, the mountain peaks were covered in snow and the contrast was remarkable. The tourist took a lot of photographs and the woman went to too many shops where she spent hours looking at various things – designer home accessories, three-dimensional children's books, silk scarves – and all the time kept asking him if he liked them. At the tiniest hint that he did not like them enough, she made a face and explained to him in detail why he had to like the object in question more than he did. They stayed in a small, very luxurious boutique hotel, even though both of them could not really afford it, and spent in Turin a total of forty-eight hours in the course of which they had sex eight times.

In Barcelona, they found a guest house in the Gothic quarter which was considerably less expensive. Summer was in full swing. The woman gladly immersed herself in the local rhythm of life which included a three-hour siesta. The tourist was not able to sleep in the afternoon. After lunch, he returned to the hostel with her and they had sex – he was so aroused that he had to move very slowly in order to avoid coming immediately, which aroused her in turn so that in the end they came together – but then he went out alone and roamed the sun-baked empty streets like a sleepwalker; there was not a single soul in sight and everything was closed. He felt like he was in a zombie film where the protagonist wakes up in hospital after a coma and discovers that everybody else is dead. The sun was fierce and the tourist bought himself a straw hat – there was no one to see him anyway. He boarded an open top bus, toured a few attractions – the park with the sculptures, the statue of Columbus, the unfinished church with the twisted towers sprouting out of the building like mutated cucumbers – and returned, exhausted, in the early evening when the whole city (including the woman in the room) was waking up, stretching lazily and preparing to enjoy the night. He took a cold shower in a futile attempt to freshen up, then they had to go out again and they spent many, many hours on the streets – she was happily dragging him from one bar to the next, ordering tapas and wine, meeting noisy groups of friends, going out to smoke, coming back, kissing him, ordering cocktails, dragging him into even stranger bars where someone was playing the guitar or the harmonica, pulling him into a dark alley where she tried to take him in her mouth, but some people appeared and they had to run before they returned to the bar and a completely different group of friends that the tourist did not remember meeting and they went to a club where he was leaning against a column and she was laughing happily on the dance floor, among flashing lights and men pressing themselves against her and kissing her on the neck, and the tourist did not realise when he had found himself in a taxi, but he woke up when she shook his shoulder and they were in front of the hotel, they went up to their room, it was dawning outside, she pushed him into the bathroom and they took a shower together, then they were on the bed and they were having sex and she came first, biting her lips and emitting brief, sharp moans, and after he came as well, he fell asleep on top of her body, still inside her, and did not feel when she had pushed him away.

They arrived in Madrid late in the evening and their next flight to Seville with the same airline was so early on the next morning that they were offered to stay in the airline hotel which was right next to the airport. She was not very enthusiastic about this, but the tourist insisted and they were taken by minibus to the hotel – a huge square monstrosity with the largest foyer that the tourist had ever seen. Their room was luxurious but indescribably featureless. After he replied yet another time that he most definitely did not want to go to downtown Madrid in the middle of the night, the tourist considered the contents of the minibar, opened two of the miniature bottles of whisky, poured them in one glass, added ice, leaned against the pillows on the bed and switched on the television set. She went inside the bathroom. When she emerged, wrapped in a towel, and started methodically applying various hair, face, hands and body lotions onto herself, he tried to pull her close but she resisted and finally told him that she was indisposed. He insisted. When he pulled out of her there was not a single drop of blood on the bed and the condom was red anyway.

They arrived in Seville just in time for the biggest festival of the year when the whole city went mad for a whole week. Nobody went out before sundown and almost nobody came home before sunrise. Everybody was wearing masks and costumes. The tourist announced that he was going to stay in the room – they checked in an ordinary hotel from a mid-level chain, the only thing going for it the proximity to the cathedral with the golden weathervane. The woman shrugged and went out. He unpacked his luggage, took a shower and went out on the balcony to have a beer or two, which was a mistake, because the evening was so hot and airless that he started sweating again. He returned to the room, switched on the air conditioning, closed the door to the balcony, watched some television and fell asleep. He woke up once, shortly before dawn. The woman was still not there. He went to sleep again.

When he woke up next, she was in the bathroom. He lay listening to the familiar noises: the water from the shower, the water in the sink, the water down the toilet. When he heard the bathroom door open, he closed his eyes and pretended he was sleeping.

He lay next to her for the next thirty minutes, then he got up and dressed, carefully keeping quiet. The woman was sleeping soundly. Her clothes were thrown on a chair and there was a domino on top of them – she must have taken part in some carnival. The tourist left her a note where to find him, walked out of the room and quietly closed the door behind him.

There had been a storm during the night. The streets were wet but quickly drying under the sun which peeked from between the roofs and promised another hot day. There were wild oranges everywhere, torn by the wind off the decorative trees on the sidewalks. There was a sharp, fresh smell in the air.

The tourist took a walk in a botanical garden, bought a newspaper, sat down on a bench, read it, completed the crossword and the logical problems and left it folded on the bench so that someone else could read it if they wanted to. Then he found a café that was serving breakfast, sat down and ate without noticing the food. He kept walking as the streets gradually came to life – with the exception of public transportation drivers, cleaners and vendors, all the people around him must have been tourists as the native population was sleeping off another festival night. Finally, he went to the square with the emblems of various Spanish provinces that he had specified in his note.

The woman was about an hour late but she came. He pointed out to her where she could buy coffee. She asked him if he wanted something. He did not. She went and came back with a tall paper cup. She sat down next to him and they watched the tourists in silence – mostly schoolchildren, going around the square, screaming and laughing.

The woman told him that she preferred to be on her own for a while. He was not surprised to hear it. In fact, he did not mind being on his own for a while as well. The woman asked him if he needed an explanation. The tourist did not need an explanation but he nodded anyway. The woman told him some things about himself. Most of them were true. He tried to feel angry or hurt, but he could not manage it. He knew just as well what was wrong with him, but he could not see what he could do. It seemed absurd to feel angry that he was not able to be happy. On the other hand, he completely – albeit theoretically – understood the woman who wanted to feel happy and share this happiness with someone. When she was finished, he suggested that they go back to the hotel. They walked in silence. She packed and left. She did not hesitate at the door, nor did she kiss him or anything like this, but at least she did not hit him with her umbrella.

The tourist was left alone in the hotel room.

After a few minutes, he went down to the reception and asked to talk to the hotel manager. The boy at the reception looked alarmed and asked him if there was a problem. The tourist shook his head. No, there was no problem at all, he was just working for a tourist website and he wanted to make a brief interview with the hotel manager that he thought to include in his review for the hotel. The hotel was fine and everything in his room was alright, thank you. Everything was alright.

The boy picked up the phone to call the manager. The tourist leaned against the reception desk and waited. He felt like drumming with his fingers on the desk but he restrained himself.

18. Lisbon

The tourist was intimidated by people who were having fun. He was pretty good when he had to lie by the pool, read books, visit restaurants, see sights and listen to guides. What he had never been able to comprehend was the gratuitous joy of other people, the sudden bursts of laughter, loud voices and energetic gesticulation.

He was sitting on a lounging chair with an open book in his lap, without turning a single page, watching the people through his dark sunglasses, expressionless. When it was time for lunch, he stood up, collected his things, went up to his room, took a shower, dressed and went down to the restaurant. He ate slowly and methodically and he had just one glass of white wine. Then he went back up to his room, lay down on his back on the bed and stared at the ceiling.

On the night before, he had tried to go to a casino. He took his most presentable shirt and jacket to the hotel basement to be taken care of, dressed carefully and took a taxi to the casino. He had chosen one of the more popular card games beforehand and had practiced a few times on his laptop – first against the computer and then on a website against real players – until he was comfortable with the rules. In spite of this, his stomach turned the minute he entered the casino. He immediately sensed that people here were having even more fun than elsewhere. Their senses seemed to be sharpened against exceptions such as himself who were not having fun.

The dealers looked at him accusingly. The waiters were bumping against him on purpose when they walked past with their trays. The other players on the tables pretended that they did not see him, but were in fact studying him with a mixture of contempt and desire to crush him in their stupid game in order to collect his chips. After thirty minutes on the table, the tourist bet everything on an unpromising hand, was relieved to lose it and left the casino, forcing himself not to run.

His room had a view to the parking lot but there was a large common balcony with a view to the ocean. The hotel was in one of those traditional Portuguese resorts, thirty minutes by train away from Lisbon, which were built two centuries back. The hotel that he was staying at was probably at least a hundred years old. In spite of all this, the tourist could not force himself to feel enough interest in the hotel to write a review. Since he had come from Seville, he felt even more dazed and passive than usual.

He slowly raised his hand in front of his face to look at his watch. The time startled him. There were four hours and thirty minutes to go before dinner time. And after dinner, there were at least three more hours before he would be able to sleep. There was no gym in the old hotel, just a pool, and the tourist had already used it before lunch. He had finished the book that he had brought with himself and there were only newspapers on sale in the hotel lobby, so he had to go to the centre of the resort to buy another one.

The tourist sat up on the bed and opened his laptop. He had started a file with the name of the hotel which was still empty. He opened the file and stared at the blinking cursor for a while, then he closed it. He closed the laptop, opened the fridge and stood in front of it for a while. He did not feel like drinking. He took a soda and went out on the balcony. The cars stood in the parking lot, baked by the sun, doing nothing. At this hour, nobody in the hotel was doing anything. Most guests were elderly people who needed a few hours' rest after lunch. If he had still been with the woman, she would have needed a few hours' rest after lunch as well, because she would have stayed up until dawn. She would have been sleeping on her belly on the bed in the room, naked, tangled in the sheets as usual, her smooth-skinned legs would have been spread diagonally to take up as much space as possible and her dishevelled black hair would have covered her face.

The tourist pressed the cold soda can against his forehead to make this thought go away, he returned to his room and closed the curtains. Then he opened his laptop once again and entered the other website.

He had not done it since that day in New York when he had received the message from the young thrill-seeker and, after chasing him across two continents to Amsterdam, he had told himself that he was not going to take any new orders. The familiar interface of the website had an unexpectedly soothing effect on him. The tourist ran a tentative search – just in case – to see what orders were placed nearby.

There was the perfect order. The woman was sixty-five years old and in her notice on the website she wrote that she had always dreamed of seeing Lisbon before she died. After she had been diagnosed with a rare, lethal cancer with minimal chances of survival and horrible side effects from any known form of therapy, she had calmly taken care of her matters and had arrived in the Portuguese capital where she remained now; enjoying what life she had left. Her request was to go without any pain or inconvenience for anyone.

The tourist closed his profile and exited the website but he could not stop thinking about the woman until the evening when he tried to start a conversation with two young women in the hotel restaurant and they coldly explained to him that he had already attempted the same thing on the previous evening and his attempt had been just as unsuccessful. The tourist blushed and retreated to the bar. They might have been telling the truth. Or not – perhaps some other grim loner who looked like him had tried to introduce himself to them. Or it was not that, either – they must have prepared this response in advance just so that they could deflect grim loners like him. He had a few more drinks, then he went up to his room by the stairs because he could not bear the thought of having a conversation with the elderly man who serviced the elevator, opened the website, took the job, closed the website, brushed his teeth and went to bed.

The streets of Lisbon, just like the streets of many other European cities frequented by tourists in this season, smelled like urine. The city seemed old and unfinished at the same time – as if they had started a restoration programme so long ago that the restoration works themselves were already antique. He took a taxi from the station to the hotel where his client was staying, and checked into a free room on her floor. Then he took a shower and went out to spend the time until dinner aimlessly roaming the meandering alleys on the old hill. He did not see anything more or different than what he had already seen in dozens of other places. Every city was like every other city. The tiny tramcars, the big elevator made of wrought iron which connected the lower city with the upper city, the tables with square cloths placed in the middle of the endless stairs that passed for streets – it felt like he had already seen even the most characteristic features of the city somewhere else. He had a small carafe of red wine in a restaurant with a view to the brightly lit castle on the opposite hill, and returned to his hotel where he went to sleep almost immediately.

During breakfast, the tourist approached the table where the woman was sitting, and asked if he could join her. She looked at him curiously but calmly and nodded at the chair opposite. She was small, with bleached blonde hair and the lightest-coloured eyes that the tourist had ever seen. Her fight with the illness could only be seen in the deep shadows under her eyes and the painful wrinkles around her mouth when she was not smiling. She was having a grapefruit for breakfast.

The tourist asked her if it was her first time in Lisbon and she said yes. Then she asked him the same question and he said no. The woman asked him what was the reason for his visit and he silently nodded in her direction before he sipped his coffee. The woman looked at him in silence and then nodded as well. Then she asked him if he had any plans for the day. The tourist replied that he was completely at her disposal.

The two of them walked out of the hotel and went down the central boulevard to a monument with a café in front. The woman was easily tired and she suggested that they sit down for a while. The tourist readily agreed. He was enjoying her company. The pleasure with which she chose a particular type of coffee from the menu and then sipped it in tiny sips was contagious. She had lived a long, interesting life and she told a good story about it, but she was also an attentive listener and asked appropriate questions, without violating his privacy or the topic about the profession that he had chosen for himself. She was a real old school lady. The tourist had never had a conversation with such a woman.

After thirty minutes she announced that she was ready to continue with the adventure. The tourist had read in his guidebook that some of the routes of the traditional trams of Lisbon could be used as an equivalent of the open top tourist buses in other cities, but with the added pleasure of watching locals in their native environment. The woman was thrilled with the idea. They boarded a tiny tramcar and rode it for hours. Sometimes they would point something outside to each other or discreetly nod at one of passengers who were getting on and off the tramcar. Sometimes, a small smile played on the woman's lips and whenever he noticed it, the tourist would also smile encouragingly.

They had lunch at the port where there were several small fish restaurants. The tourist suggested white wine but the woman regretfully declined – she was on very strong medication to be able to get out of bed at all, and she did not want to risk spending the rest of the day in a coma. He did not order alcohol, either – he had a soda even though she insisted that he did not defer to her.

After lunch, they went to a nearby post station – in this city, even the post stations looked like elegantly aged architectural monuments – and the woman sent a few postcards to various destinations all over the world. The tourist helped her choose the postcards and agreed that there was nothing more beautiful and personal than sending a postcard in this day and age.

Later, they had ice cream. The tourist could not remember when he had last had ice cream.

They were planning dinner when the woman's face was suddenly tight with pain and they had to sit down on a bench because she could not go on. The tourist was worried when he looked at her: it seemed like a completely different human being was sitting next to him, exhausted and broken beyond repair. She sat with her eyes closed for a while, resting her head on the back of the bench. Then she cautiously stood up and announced that the fit was over but it was perhaps better that they returned to the hotel. She could not ride a taxi or any other vehicle because she was worried that she was going to be motion sick, so they had to walk back, which took several hours. Some of the people on the street would give them a look when they passed them by – they were walking that slowly – but then quickly looked away, embarrassed by their own morbid curiosity. The woman did not notice them. After a while, the tourist stopped noticing them, too.

He walked her to her room but did not accept the invitation to come in. He was going to come back later that night to complete the order and they both knew it. It was better to say goodbye properly now. The two of them stood by the door in silence for a while. Then the woman asked him why he was so unhappy. The tourist replied that he did not know. The woman made a sound and in the yellow dusk of the ancient chandelier in the corridor, it took him a while to realise that she was laughing quietly. The tourist uncertainly smiled. The woman pointed out that perhaps it was nothing to wonder about, as he communicated only with people who had decided to end their own lives. She thought that perhaps all human emotions were contagious. Perhaps he had to meet someone who had decided to start something new.

The tourist did not say anything.

The woman leaned against the door and asked him if she had already told him that she had been a professional tennis player about forty years ago. The tourist shook his head. The woman smiled to herself and told him about a game that she considered the most important game in her career. She had lost the first set and the first three games of the second. Her opponent had been much better and even though she had put up a furious resistance in the beginning, during the second set she had lost her will to play and all hope that she could turn the match, so she had just been waiting for the punishment to be over with. The woman was serving in the fourth game of the second set, but her opponent was, nevertheless, winning it with love-forty. And then something happened, something that had never happened to her during a match – and it happened rarely even during training sessions. When she served next, she felt her racket, the ball and a certain spot on the other side of the net connect, as if they were on an invisible line and she could not have hit the ball outside it even if she had wanted to. It was an ace. Her opponent managed to return some of her next serves, but the supernatural sensation of being one with the court continued and she was able to claw back to deuce, won two advantages in a row and the game.

The woman was silent. The tourist waited a little and then asked her if she had finally won the match, as well. The woman laughed and shook her head. Of course, she had lost the match. But during this game she had learned that every game is a new game, no matter what happened before it.

The tourist hesitated some more, then he wished her goodnight. The woman nodded and told him that she was going to leave the door unlocked. He nodded as well, turned and walked away down the corridor.

19. Reykjavik

The tourist was surprised by the size of Reykjavik. He knew that the total population of Iceland was three hundred thousand people and half of them lived in the capital, but all the same he did not expect a single main street about a kilometre long, with two or three side streets lined with shops and bars. He walked up to the modernist church on the hill and walked back down to the centre of the city where he walked around the lake once, looking at the thousands of birds above the water. He found a golf ball in the grass and he put it in his pocket without thinking about it. Then he walked back out on the main street and walked down the whole length of the street once more.

People looked good and had amazing haircuts – both men and women. (One of the side streets seemed to consist entirely of hairdressing salons.) When the tourist was silent, they spoke quickly in their absolutely incomprehensible language, but whenever he asked anybody about something, all the people in the place switched to English so that he would not feel uncomfortable. Their English was also very good.

He liked the city as well. There were a few tall buildings in the centre, but most houses along the main street were on two floors and looked like film sets – with brightly coloured walls and blindingly white windowsills.

The tourist ate dinner in a pub – the food was Scandinavian, with lots of fried and breaded things and tasteless vegetables – and was surprised at how expensive everything was. He knew that in a couple of days he would get used to the local currency and would not pay attention to the prices anymore – what else could he do – but at the beginning, he automatically calculated everything in euros and the price of a pint seemed appalling. No wonder so few people lived here.

After dinner, he visited several bars but they were all half-empty. A bartender that he started talking to explained how things were done in Reykjavik: no one would go out on a week night, but on Friday and Saturday they would all be out until the morning, zealously upholding the local tradition of the bar crawl. The man pronounced it in such a way that the last word seemed to be used quite literally. The tourist asked to try some local alcohol. The bartender replied that this was not a very good idea. The tourist insisted, the bartender shrugged and poured him a clear drink in a shot glass, serving it on a saucer with a piece of dried fish. The tourist downed the drink. It tasted like old sunflower seed oil that had a chilli pepper soaked in it. The fish tasted like wallpaper glue, but at least it did help him not to throw up the drink, as the bartender had promised.

When he came out of the bar, the sun was low above the horizon and its bright slanting rays were basking everything around in deep, rich colours. He squinted and looked at his watch. It was eleven in the evening. The tourist put on his sunglasses and started walking along the seaside alley towards the hotel. It was quiet. There were people in tracksuits and earphones jogging along the alley. The tourist felt like it was early morning, and he felt a little embarrassed by the fact that he was drunk.

Around midnight, he sat down on a bench in the golden light of the night and watched the sea. There was a modernist steel sculpture on the beach and after staring at it for some time, he recognised the stylised silhouette of a Viking ship. In a few minutes, a man who was even more drunk than him approached the bench. They talked for a while, even though the tourist could not understand anything the man was saying. If he had to guess, they were talking about the seagulls. Then the man left, singing to himself.

The tourist crawled back to the hotel, went up to his room, closed the heavy wooden shutters on the windows and pulled the blinds down to make the room dark enough to sleep in.

He did not remember getting undressed to go to bed, but in the morning he woke up in his underwear under the sheets. The taste in his mouth was not particularly unpleasant, which meant that he had probably managed to brush his teeth, as well. He felt unexpectedly rested, although when he pulled up the blinds and opened the shutters, the sun looked like it was in the same spot in the sky and he had a moment of déjà vu that made him feel sick for a minute.

It was only at the airport, while he was slowly sipping a Bloody Mary and watching the plane of the Icelandic airline being prepared to take the passengers that the tourist realised he had been looking at the island in a different way the whole time. Usually, he looked for something to catch his eye so that he could write a short, clever piece and continue as quickly as possible towards the next destination and the next order, leaving no trace.

But if he was not mistaken, for the past few days he had been looking for a place to stay.

20. Copenhagen

The tourist was not expecting to like Sweden, but as soon as he arrived at the airport, he sensed the allure of Scandinavian design combined with a large number of tall, beautiful and well-behaved people who had grown up with Scandinavian design all around. Stockholm was an urban fairytale of parks, island and impeccable public transportation. There was a large natural reserve right in the middle of the city where wolves, otters and bears looked like they were feeling at home.

The tourist stayed for several days in which he was eating well and going to bed early. Then he continued towards Gothenburg (same as Stockholm, with ships) and Malmo (same as Gothenburg, with added fantastic skyscraper towering above the port like a tornado of glass and steel). He travelled on buses which he reserved on the internet and received the tickets for as text messages on his mobile phone. For some reason, the buses were all leaving in fantastically early hours. Riding the bus from Gothenburg to Malmo, the tourist fell asleep and when he woke up, he saw an empty road among the pine woods, with a single dark-blue Volvo going in the opposite direction that was so old that he had had the same model toy car as a child. Riding on the bus from Malmo to Copenhagen across the bridge, the tourist fell asleep again and when he woke up, he saw the gigantic wind turbines in the sea far off the bridge – they were so majestic that the tanker passing between two of them looked tiny as a toy.

The Copenhagen hotel that he had accepted the order to write about was brand new but it had already won a number of design, innovation and ecological awards. There was no reception desk – instead, there was a line of identical consoles with an interface which encouraged the guests to check themselves in. The tourist typed in his information and the machine welcomed him before it spat out a key card with the number of his room. The room was operated by a touchscreen remote control which regulated temperature, the brightness and colour of lighting and the musical background. There was a flat screen display above the bed which offered a variety of audio programmes, video games, television channels and films. The tourist felt like he was in a spaceship – or rather, a spaceship from a nineteen seventies science-fiction film. He played a few games on the screen (the room beat him at chess, but he was better at backgammon), then he opened his laptop and wrote a review in which he proposed that the tourist board of Copenhagen should seriously consider legal action against this hotel as the guests might never leave their rooms to visit the other tourist attractions. He sent the review (naturally, the room had broadband wireless connection), closed the laptop, and looked around for a minibar. Either there was none or it was designed so cleverly that he was not able to find it. Clearly, in the future no one was going to drink.

He stayed in Copenhagen for two days. The city looked like a Mediterranean tourist capital, only smaller and more orderly. He supposed that it would not be the same in winter, but right now it was quite nice. On the evening before he left, he sat down in a pub near his hotel where a bearded man was singing and strumming a guitar on the small stage. He had a few beers, but the young women at the next table had obviously had a few more as they noisily moved to his table and insisted that he tell them something interesting about himself. The tourist tried to leave, but the girls ordered another beer for him, and the nearest one asked him what he was doing. He replied that he was writing a book. She seemed impressed (or at least, ready to feel somewhat impressed), but right then the guitar player said hello to the girls from the stage and they immediately lost all interest in the tourist. He stood up, relieved, sneaked out of the pub, and returned to his hotel where he had a large selection of films to watch.

On the plane to Warsaw, he thought about what he had said to the young woman in Copenhagen. He could probably really write a book if he decided to. The tourist website that he worked for was naturally owned by a larger publishing company. He could collect the more successful hotel reviews that he had written in the past few years and organise them into something like a guidebook. Or he could start with a clean slate and write a guidebook or a travelogue. He was certainly qualified enough to do it.

Warsaw was not what he had imagined. There was an old part of the city, but the history of the old part was nonsensical: after the medieval buildings and streets were demolished during the Second World War, socialist Poland had decided to restore the whole neighbourhood brick by brick, using preserved building plans and photographs of the original buildings. They had employed various technologies for artificial aging of the building materials which had been cutting-edge at the time. This was an oxymoron on so many different levels that the tourist gave up on analysing them and ordered another beer.

Krakow was a little better. At least the historical centre of the city was really historical. It was raining hard all the time, though, and the tourist caught a cold so he sneezed and coughed all the way on the train to Budapest (which seemed a very unpleasant place for all that people said about it) and Ljubljana (where he started to feel better, the skies cleared and all people seemed to have straw-blond hair and tiny snub noses). He stayed for a few days in Ljubljana (there was energetic night life but not much else) and continued on to Zagreb.

Where he promptly fell in love.

21. Zagreb

The guest house was in the centre of the old town, at the end of a little street at the bottom of a hill. The tourist arrived very late in the evening and did not see much of the city from the taxi – a highway from the airport, bathed in yellow lights, which transformed into a series of narrower and more winding streets. There was a young woman with lots of jet-black curly hair at the reception who wrote down his information and gave him the key. He was so exhausted that after he went up to his room, he did not have enough energy for a shower, so he simply undressed and crawled under the covers.

He woke up to the sound of church bells. In the light of day, his room looked tiny, like the dwelling of a dwarf from a fairytale. There was old wooden furniture repainted in white. Instead of a wardrobe, there was a big chest that he had left his bag on last night. The window was large and round, with a view to the fantastic roof of a church, covered in white, red and blue tiles arranged to form the coat of arms of the city.

The tourist got up, took a shower, brushed his teeth, shaved, and went down to the reception area which looked more like a living room. The house was on two floors and he figured that it had three or four guest rooms such as his. In the living room, there was a sofa and a low table with a few board games and an almost finished jigsaw puzzle on it. Behind the reception desk was the same girl who had met him last night.

In the light of day he could see that her eyes were brightly, almost impossibly blue.

The tourist explained that he was writing hotel reviews and she was happy to show him around the guest house. The bedrooms were on the second floor and there was a small bar on the first floor, straight in from the living room, and an even smaller flower shop next to the bar which also sold handmade jewellery. There was no one in the shop. The girl explained that she was working the shop, as well – there was a tiny bell hanging on the inside of the door so that she could hear it from the reception when a customer entered the shop. Afterwards, they returned to the living room and she offered to make coffee. The tourist accepted. He could not take his eyes off her. She asked him what he was going to write about her hotel. The tourist replied that he wanted to write an ode instead of a review. The girl laughed. When she asked him how long he was going to stay, he replied that he did not know but it would probably be long. She nodded and smiled. She did not seem surprised.

After he finished his coffee, the tourist went out to see the town. It was Saturday and the girl had explained to him that everyone was going out with their families for walk around the centre of the town, then they were shopping together in the town market and finally returning home to prepare lunch. The tourist decided that this was a charming tradition. He liked the people, too. The older ones looked like the old people from his childhood, the ones that visited his parents and pinched his cheeks, and the younger ones looked self-confident but in a good way. The tourist felt at home. He was not quite certain where Zagreb was on the map, but he was most probably born less than a thousand kilometres from here.

Passing through the market, the tourist impulsively bought a bunch of marigolds from a smiling old woman with a headscarf and a face wrinkled like a dry apple. Walking back to the guest house, he remembered that the girl was selling flowers, too, so the marigolds were a rather stupid idea, but he did not want to throw them away.

When he returned, the girl was not there. She had left a note – presumably for him, as there were no other guests in the house – that she was out to the shops and she was going to be back in the afternoon. The tourist found a vase to put the flowers in, went up to his room with the round window and opened his laptop. There was a new message on his profile on the tourist website. A hotel in a Croatian resort on the Adriatic coast had contacted the tourist website to ask for a review. He checked out the website of the hotel – it was part of a local chain which also owned clubs and restaurants – and decided to take the order. He had to work something. Besides, if the hotel was good and they liked his review, he could write about their other places as well. He knew of people who had made the move from reviewing hotels to joining the other side and were now working as public relations managers or advertising directors for various hotel chains. In this way, he would have a more stable job which would allow him to stay and live here longer. The tourist reminded himself not to rush it, but in the bright light of the day and in this house where everything had been touched by her, it was difficult not to think about the future.

He packed his bag, went down and added a sentence to the girl's note to tell her that he was going to come back tomorrow. Then he walked out, went to the central square of the old town and found the office of an international rental car agency. Thirty minutes later, he was already driving out of town, with the windows open. Ninety minutes after that, he reached the seaside resort where the hotel was located.

The resort was horrendous. It was one of those projects inflated by the construction boom, growing like tumours all along the coast in South Europe, only to go bankrupt, desolate and dilapidated a few years later. The tourist had seen similar resorts in Spain and it looked like the sickness was spreading east. Most hotels were not completed and there was furious construction work going on, the air was thick with the boom of heavy machinery and dust. The alleys of the resort were smashed beyond belief by the wheels of the heavy trucks. The sea was almost invisible behind the hotels packed tightly next to each other on the beach.

The tourist found the hotel and parked his small rented car on a trampled, yellowing lawn which obviously served as a parking lot, next to a German sports car that looked like it was about to transform into an alien robot any minute. Then he took his bag and entered the lobby.

On the inside, the hotel looked like every cent that had been spared on infrastructure had been invested in decoration. They had a fountain with crystal dolphins and swans, merrily playing with each other, clearly unconcerned that this could have never happened in nature. They had a gigantic chandelier of the type that breaks off and falls on top of the bad guy in an action film just when things look desperate for the good guy. What they did not have was a doorman – the tourist had to put all his strength into opening the massive door.

The young man behind the reception desk was watching him with a mixture of boredom and idle curiosity. The tourist approached him and announced that he had reserved a room in the hotel. The young man typed something in his computer and the computer immediately crashed. The young man said something in Croatian that sounded like it could not have been anything other than a curse, and wrote down his information in a thick tattered notebook with a cheap plastic pen. Then he gave him the key card for the room and wished him a pleasant stay.

The elevator was not working. The tourist took the stairs and found that his key card was not working, either. He walked down the stairs back to the reception desk where the young man assured him that this was absolutely impossible and demonstrated to him the exact way in which he was supposed to swipe the key card through the slot of the lock in order to open it. The tourist pointed out that this was not the first time that he was using a key card. In his turn, the receptionist pointed out that this was not the first time a guest could not open the door of his room, but with some persistence the key card was going to do what it was made to do. The tourist walked back up the stairs and again could not open his door. He was starting to go mad. He dropped his bag on the floor, carefully put the key card in the slot and swiped it as slowly and tightly as if he was trying to cut the lock in two. The door clicked and opened.

His room was small, irregular-shaped and looked straight onto the balconies of another hotel built approximately three metres away from this one. In fact, it was not built – it was being built right now, and there was a guy on the opposite balcony, with a folded newspaper for a hat and a cigarette hanging from his mouth, who was putting up tiles and listening to a small radio. The tourist closed the door of his own balcony so that he could not hear the music and pulled the curtains so that he could not see the working guy. In this way, he had the opportunity to discover that his room smelled like fresh paint.

He walked into the bathroom to have a shower. The bracket on the wall which held the showerhead so that the water could be directed was loose, and no matter what he did, the showerhead gradually tilted down under its own weight and the water started splashing against the wall. In addition, the water kept going colder and colder, even though the tourist kept increasing the flow from the hot faucet – right until the moment when it started to go hotter and hotter, even though he kept increasing the flow from the cold faucet. The complimentary shampoo inexplicably smelled like cooked vegetables.

The tourist went down to the reception. The young man was not thrilled to see him. The tourist asked if it was possible to meet the hotel manager. The young man replied that he doubted it. The tourist explained that he was asked to write a review about this hotel for the international tourist website that he was working for and he really insisted on meeting the hotel manager. The young man shrugged as if he wanted to say that he had done everything in his powers to prevent the meeting, dug a mobile phone out of his pocket and called someone. He had a brief conversation, cut the connection and returned to his computer. The tourist leaned over the reception desk to look at the computer screen. It displayed an unfinished game of solitaire. The tourist inquired after the result of the phone conversation. The young man replied that the boss would be there in a minute, no longer trying to sound polite.

The tourist waited. Ten minutes passed. Then a big man of about fifty years appeared out of a corridor, wearing white trousers and a white shirt open at the neck. He had grizzled hair, thick eyebrows, heavy gold rings on his fingers and fat lips. A cigarette was burning between the fingers of his right hand. He stuck the cigarette in his mouth to give the tourist's hand a firm shake and motioned for the tourist to follow him. They went to the bar at the other end of the lobby. A subservient waitress brought an espresso for the hotel manager. The tourist did not want anything.

He explained to the manager that at this point, he had two options: he could either write a negative review or write nothing at all. In both cases, he recommended that the manager contacted an advertising agency instead of an independent website which evaluated hotels. The man stubbed out his cigarette, squinting against the smoke. Then he explained to the tourist that in fact, he was not just the manager but the owner of this hotel. In his view, his hotel was one of the best in the resort (the tourist interrupted him to point out that this was not saying much), so if the tourist had a problem with his room or something like that, he could have just asked to see him so that the problem could be solved, instead of acting like a little bitch.

The tourist thought that he had not heard right. The man repeated the last word. He was sitting opposite the tourist in the low, heavy armchair with leather upholstery, looking at him. The tourist looked back at him, but could not meet his eyes and looked away. He could very well imagine the same conversation being conducted in a basement where he would be tied with cable to the chair and the white shirt of the hotel owner would be spattered with blood. The man asked him what he intended to do now. The tourist replied that it was probably best if he left now, and he would think carefully before he did something. The hotel owner advised him to think very carefully. The tourist nodded. The man suddenly smiled and reached over the low table to pat him on the shoulder. He had a very heavy hand. There were grizzled hairs on the top side of his fat fingers.

The tourist went up to his room, took his bag and walked back down. The hotel owner was on his mobile phone, but when he saw him, he grinned again and pointed his forefinger at the tourist like it was a gun. The tourist nodded again and left.

Driving back to Zagreb, he thought about what he really ought to do. He was on the Balkans, after all, so there should be a wide range of opportunities.

Naturally, eliminating the owner did not mean that the hotel was going to get better by itself. Besides, there were so many other hotels in which ordinary people were paying to be cheated and humiliated instead of spending a few of the best days in their lives...

But then again, he had to start somewhere.

PART THREE

22. Edinburgh

The tourist had never gotten used to guns. They seemed as dangerous to use as they were for the victim. In addition, they brought about too many complications, as he had to fly all the time and he never carried anything more than hand luggage. He could not even imagine the trouble of procuring a gun everywhere that he arrived to do a job. The troubles which resulted from his alibi profession – a lonely and boring life in hotel rooms; his health ruined by constant travel and jet lag – were more than enough.

So he had to improvise.

He sat down on the edge of the road and leaned back on the low concrete wall of the highway crossing, his back to the highway five or six metres below. He had arrived on a local bus a few hours ago, he had gotten off on the only stop in the nearest small town and he had walked here on the third class road which had more potholes than asphalt. The only vehicle that he met on the way was a horse-drawn cart. The horse looked exhausted and desperate and there were flies all over its eyelids and nostrils that it was not even trying to shake off. Since the tourist had stood on the crossing above the highway, not a single car had passed by on the road, but he looked both ways just in case. There was nothing but quickly gathering dusk everywhere he looked.

Unlike the third class road, the highway was very much used. It had six lanes, three in every direction, divided by a containing wall. Traffic was heavier in one direction – sitting in this way, the tourist was able to see several kilometres along the highway and the lanes looked like three almost continuous white streams of car lights. He was facing Zagreb and his back was turned to the disgusting seaside resort with the hotel which he had been supposed to write about. Traffic from the resort to the capital was very much lighter – the three lanes looked darker by the minute, dotted with the occasional bright red of brake lights. It was Friday. Nobody drives back from a seaside resort on a Friday evening. The heavy traffic from the capital to the resort was explained by the large number of people planning to spend the weekend in it. Some of them might even stay in the hotel that the tourist had never written a review about, after the manager had advised him to think very carefully before he did anything.

And the tourist really thought about it. He thought for several days in which he drove from the capital to the seaside resort and back in a rental car, parking a short distance away from the hotel and watching it. After he had established the evening hour in which the hotel manager left, got in his unnecessarily powerful German sports car and drove off to the capital with an unnecessarily high speed, the tourist returned to his room, opened his laptop and used a map to make a very simple calculation. He had noticed the highway crossing with the third class road above on his way back from the resort and he had remembered something that he had seen on the news.

Which is why he glanced at his watch now, turned around and stood on his knees, leaning on the low concrete wall of the crossing, facing the three lanes of the highway which led from the resort to the capital. He placed his elbows on the edge of the wall and started watching the traffic with the small binoculars that he had bought earlier in the day. He had leather gloves on even though he hardly needed them. By his feet was an irregularly shaped stone as big as a bowling ball that the tourist had found by the third class road a few hundred metres away from this spot and had carried over in his backpack.

He was guessing that the hotel manager would be driving in the fastest lane of the highway and he was right. After he had seen a few cars that were not his, the tourist recognised the make and model and even managed to see with his binoculars the last number of the registration plate that he had remembered. The car was approaching at approximately one hundred and sixty kilometres per hour. The tourist put down the binoculars, used both hands to pick up the stone and rested it against the edge of the wall. He was certain that the drivers in the cars on the highway could not see him – the resort was west of Zagreb so the silhouette of the tourist was not outlined against the darkening sky in the east. The only unknown factor was the possibility that the hotel manager would decide to change the lane – the tourist knew that in this case he would not be able to move quickly enough to change his position before the car passed by below the crossing. Of course, then he would just have to come back tomorrow.

He did not have to.

The second calculation that he had done was a little more complicated, but it was still not rocket science. He had used the timer in his mobile phone to record the time in which the small stones that he had been dropping from the crossing when there were no cars on the highway below, reached the surface of the road. (And he knew that in spite of his intuitive feeling about it, the heavier stone would fall with the same velocity.) Waiting for the hotel manager's car, he had tracked enough other cars to calculate the average time it took them to approach, and he had noted a milestone painted in white which seemed to glow in the dusk about fifty metres away from the highway crossing.

Just as the hotel manager's car passed by the milestone, the tourist pushed the stone off the edge of the wall.

He did not see exactly what happened, but when the car shot out from under the crossing on the opposite side, it was no longer moving in the same lane. Instead, it was crossing the highway diagonally to the right and simultaneously skidding anticlockwise. A second later, inertia overcame the force of gravity and the car flipped over.

The tourist had seen a documentary in which the stunts director of the latest film about the exploits of the famous secret agent explained how difficult it was to make a similar car flip over without the use of additional jet propulsion charges mounted under the chassis. Now he thought that the stunts director must have been trying to make his job look harder than it was, because he clearly saw the hotel manager's car flip over a total of six times, soaring over the edge of the road and the deep concrete ditch on the right side of the highway and rolling off through the empty field, meanwhile looking less and less like a car and more and more like something very crumpled. When it finally ground to a stop, the few cars on his side of the highway had stopped and excited people were coming out of them, and most of the cars on the other side of the highway were slowing down to get a look at what was going on. The tourist was hoping that their curiosity would not bring about additional, even though not so dramatic, car crashes.

If he had been hoping for an explosion, he was disappointed.

He waited a few more minutes for it to get completely dark. Now he could not see the crumpled car even with the help of his binoculars, but it was quite clear that it would take emergency teams with metal cutters to extract what was left of the hotel manager out of the car.

The tourist shuddered. It was hideously easy to accomplish. Now he was going to develop a phobia of driving on a highway, in addition to his phobia of flying. He shrugged, stood up, took off his gloves, and started walking back to the bus stop in the little town.

They had rented the apartment in Edinburgh for a whole month. The tourist could not believe that anyone would volunteer to spend a whole month with him anywhere, but his new girlfriend was adamant that there was no point in going anywhere for less. From the very start of their relationship, when she entered his room in her guest house that the tourist was staying in, it was established that she knew better.

The apartment looked like it was built for hobbits: it was partially underground, at the end of a quiet little street not far from the centre of the city, and everything in it looked smaller than generally accepted, except for the fridge. His girlfriend organised an expedition to the nearest supermarket to fill the fridge with food. The tourist could not remember the last time he had been in a supermarket to buy food. They settled down in the apartment, they slept in late, and his girlfriend went to the fridge and back in her underwear to prepare improvised, sumptuous snacks in all hours. They made love all the time. They had an unspoken agreement that whenever someone woke up in the night (it was usually him), they had to wake up the other person so that they could make love again before they went to sleep.

At the end of the first week, the tourist wrote a review about the rental apartment (a short story about a family of foxes, in the style of the classic English writers for children from the nineteenth century) and sent it to the tourist website, but apart from that, he had no desire to work or travel. His girlfriend's desire to devour life without ever analysing it was contagious. He was sleeping well. In the mornings, he had coffee with milk. He was still waking up at unusual hours, but at least he was not covered in cold sweat and his heartbeat slowed down in a few minutes, after he had carefully put his arm around her.

His girlfriend had a very eclectic taste in tourist attractions. They made sandwiches and went to see the tiny bronze statue of the terrier which had continued coming to the grave of his master for fourteen years after the man had been dead. They climbed up to the stone throne on the peak of the tiny mountain which rose straight from the centre of the city. They took a ferry boat to a tiny island and on the way back, his girlfriend bought a loaf of bread from the small shop at the port and taught him how to throw the bread from the stern of the ship so that the seagulls flying behind it could snatch the bread out of the air.

Sometimes, he wanted to tell her everything about himself but he never did.

His girlfriend had heard about a bookstore in Edinburgh which specialised in fairytales (somehow, his girlfriend had always heard about such things) and they walked around all day until they found it. There was a café inside and the tourist sat down to read a few international newspapers while she was browsing in the bookstore. Of course, there was nothing in the newspapers which related to his life in any way. They walked out of the bookstore holding hands.

The tourist hesitated, blinked and slowed down when he remembered where he was. He had been here, exactly on this spot, under this very stone arch gone green with the damp, where one could see the square like this and the street turned up towards the castle like that. His girlfriend turned to him with a smile and hesitated. The tourist let go of her hand to rest his hands on his knees. He told her that he was going to be alright. He asked her to go back to the café to check if he had not forgotten something in it.

But he had not forgotten a damn thing.

The boy hated travelling. He got sick on a bus. (His family did not have a car but the boy did not doubt that he was going to be sick in a car, too, if he had the chance.) He had a mortal fear of airplanes. (After the only flight he had ever taken, on an ancient Soviet plane with propellers which was about as big as a bus and shook and stank just as bad.) He liked hotel rooms, but his father was snoring so loudly that the boy and his mother were forced to resort to small clever tactics – for example, going to bed an hour earlier so that they could have at least a little sleep before the beastly sounds woke the boy up to yet another night that he was going to spend staring at the ceiling and thinking dark thoughts. (At home, they slept in separate rooms.) But most of all, he hated the helpless feeling that he did not know where he was.

And how he had gotten lost in Edinburgh about ten minutes after he had walked out of their hotel.

It had all started innocuously enough: after lunch, his parents were suddenly taken with a suspicious desire to have a nap and a dubious eagerness to allow the boy not to join them in it. The boy had already found himself in similar awkward situations before and knew from experience that there was no point in asking questions, arguing or offering alternative ways to pass the time. At first, his parents would deflect all this with strange, sly smiles and glances at each other, then they would start to get angry. In any case, he preferred them in this inexplicable sleepy mode to them shouting and slamming doors at night while the boy was lying on the bed in his room, squinting his eyes shut. Two weeks prior to their unexpected trip to Edinburgh, the boy's father had not come home all night and for the next few days, his mother walked around like a ghost and the two of them were not talking to each other at all, but compensated it with a marked, maddening kindness to the boy itself. The boy assumed that their sudden interest in the Edinburgh festival was some kind of an attempt to reconcile with each other and everything seemed to be proceeding as planned.

The boy had walked out of the hotel and up the narrow street which led to the main street. They always walked this way when they went out together. His plan was to walk a little distance up the street before he turned around and walked back the same way. The boy had a watch with a cartoon character on the face and he planned to complete this part in ten minutes. Then he planned to repeat the same exercise, only this time with an additional walk down along the main street and then back up the main street and down along the narrow street, in twenty more minutes. The boy thought that after thirty minutes, it would be alright for him to return to the hotel.

But ten minutes later, he had no idea where he was. He walked some way and back, but the narrow street looked unfamiliar and when he walked a little down the narrow street to see where it was going, he was quietly horrified to discover that it was not the same as before. He walked back up to the main street and started going this way and that to find the narrow street, but he had not remembered any landmarks and all five hundred thousand visitors of the festival expected to arrive in Edinburgh this summer according to his father's guidebook seemed to be going up and down the main street at this very moment. A lot of them were exhilarated and smelled of alcohol, waved about their large hands holding burning cigarettes and shouted out to each other so loudly that the boy jumped. There were sudden improvised theatrical and musical performances right in the middle of the street and a loud, dense crowd where there was none before, so that the boy could not push his way through, and then just as suddenly all the people were dispersing in all directions, towards the next show, and left him even more confused than before. He darted between the legs of a man on stilts; he went pale and at the last possible moment stepped out of the way of another man who breathed out fire; he bumped into a third man painted to resemble a bronze statue and the man remained completely motionless but his eyes turned on the boy with menace.

The boy huddled in a corner, under a stone arch gone green with the damp, and began to cry.

Quite some time passed before anyone paid him any attention. At first, it was a big man with stupid blue eyes, a red face and wet lips who leaned over the boy and asked him something in his own language. The boy did not understand him and cried even harder. The man uncertainly tried to make the boy calm down and in the meantime they were joined by the mother of a family with three children who stayed a few paces away with their father, looking at the boy with contempt. The mother asked him something as well, then a few more people appeared and they all began to croak something to him in their incomprehensible, ugly language.

The boy, breathless with all the crying, managed to sob out the word "hotel" that he was hoping was the same in all languages. He had to repeat it several times, but even after they finally understood him, some of the adults rolled their eyes in desperation and others openly laughed at him.

The boy did not see anything funny. He had not forgotten the previous time when he had gotten lost in some seaside resort and he had soiled his pants before he found the restaurant where he had been having dinner with his parents, quite by chance. (His mother got up from the table, grabbed his hand quite firmly and dragged him off to the ladies' room to wash him; when they returned to the table, his father sniffed at the air, made a face and they left without finishing their dinner, but they still had to pay for it.)

If he was not mistaken, there was a distinct possibility for the same thing happening now as well.

Some of the people were giving up on helping him and leaving but they were replaced by others so that the crowd around him was still quite impressive when his father finally made his way through the strangers, saw him, sighed, slapped him on the face and picked him up on his shoulders, checking to see if his pants were dry first.

On the next day, they took the bus to Loch Ness to see the monster. The boy did not see the monster but he got sick on the bus. When they arrived at the lake, they passed through a tunnel under the road, guarded by two plastic monsters, stood in line for a while and finally boarded a boat which sailed to the middle of the lake, turned a small circle and sailed back. Then they had to get on the bus again, but it was already so late that the boy fell asleep and did not wake up until they had reached the hotel.

On the next day, his mother insisted to visit some historical alley under the ground where one could see how people had been living in Edinburgh a long time ago, while his father insisted to visit the big castle on top of the city where there was going to be a military parade with drummers. The alley was claustrophobically narrow and bathed in a sinister red glow, with the gaunt shadows of the residents outlined against the black gaping doors, forever trapped in unfathomable misery. In the castle, there were a million military bands with drums enthusiastically rumbling away as if it was the end of the world.

On the next day, they went to the museum of whisky, even though the boy and his mother did not want to. There was a small artificial river inside with boats that the visitors boarded to sail through the whole museum and witness the mysterious manufacturing processes. The boat was not so bad, but afterwards they took them to a small tasting room where a man with very red cheeks and glistening eyes encouraged the grownups to try various kinds of whisky to discover the difference between them. His father tried all the kinds of whisky and was visibly swaying, murmuring to himself and spitting on the pavement as they were walking back to the hotel. When they returned to their room, his mother and his father started shouting to each other and it was the first time that the boy saw his father hit his mother. He did not hit her that hard – perhaps as hard as the slap across the face of the boy himself when he had gotten lost two days ago – but his mother froze like a statue and her face became very white, except for the imprint of his father's fingers. There was a silence, then his father reached for his mother a second time, but it was never clear whether he wanted to hit her again or hold her, because his mother sharply raised her hand in front of her face, looking in his father's eyes with fury and horror, his father stepped back and his mother went out of their hotel room. The boy went to bed and did not realise when his mother had come back, nor when his father had left, but in the morning it was only his mother on the bed and his father was gone.

The boy and his mother returned home. When the school year started, one of the first things the boys and girls had to do was to write about how they had spent the holidays. The boy wrote a story about Edinburgh in which he described it exactly as he had seen it. (He omitted only the last night when his father had hit his mother and then left them.) The boy had definitely not enjoyed this trip and did not even try to hide this when he wrote his homework. He told everything as it had been: the drunken visitors of the festival, the deafening drums, the underground alley with the ghosts from the past, and the lake which did not have a monster in it.

He got his first ever "A".

23. Baden-Wurttemberg

The tourist did not like dogs. Of course, he had never even given a thought to keeping a pet (where would he keep it, anyway?), but dogs seemed even more problematic and demanding than other species. He was left with the impression that people thought of them as members of their families, and he had no family; and the attention and maintenance that they demanded seemed like an absurd investment of time, time that he could otherwise use to read a book or something.

In spite of all this, he liked Felix. He was a small black poodle, a knot of nervous energy, waiting for them at the central station in Stuttgart together with a man who was the tourist's age and his ten-year-old daughter. The man was the husband of his girlfriend's older sister and the little girl was her niece. Felix was their dog, even though the tourist thought that his name was better suited to a cat. As they walked through the underground parking lot of the station, conversing in an erratic, uncertain mix of languages which none of the others could understand very well (the man was German and his daughter had been born here, but the tourist and his girlfriend knew very little German; in addition, the little girl knew Croatian, i.e. her mother's language, which she spoke badly and with a German accent, but the tourist could barely understand it, as well as her father; the tourist and his girlfriend spoke English to each other, but the German husband had very limited listening and completely nonexistent speaking skills in it, while the little girl had just started learning the language), Felix was alternating a dignified trot, scanning the shadows with the militant concentration of a Roman centurion, with implausibly high leaps up to their faces, trying to lick them mid-flight. It was difficult for anyone not to like him.

His girlfriend's sister's family lived in a tidy little town about twenty kilometres out of Stuttgart, in a house on three floors. The husband was a travelling representative of a biotechnological concern and covered several thousand kilometres a week in his company car to meet the representatives of other companies which might be interested in their products. He looked as exhausted as if he would never be able to recover completely. His home and his family were his sanctuary. The tourist understood him very well, except for the part with the home and the family.

Felix was also present at the late family dinner, standing next to each of the seated humans in turn, gazing at them with heartbreaking tenderness and nudging their legs with his front paw every once in a while to get something to eat. The hosts explained that their dog was addicted to cheese and human food in general and he should not be fed from the table under any circumstances; then everyone started giving him little pieces of their own food, mostly cheese. Felix would always sniff very carefully at the food before he delicately picked it with his teeth out of their hands.

When they were finished, it was already quite late, and the husband of his girlfriend's sister asked them to walk Felix while he and his wife prepared the guest bedroom. The tourist and his girlfriend walked out in the dark, quiet, empty little town. There were no cars on the streets. They did not meet anyone else except a neighbour who was walking her dog as well. The two dogs knew each other. The tourist, his girlfriend and the neighbour stopped to let Felix and the other dog complete the ritual of sniffing, going around each other and wagging their tails which clearly stood for small talk with dogs. On the way back, the tourist was holding the leash of the dog. He had never held a dog on a leash. It was an intriguing sensation.

The next day was Saturday and after they had breakfast and left Felix with the neighbour, they all boarded the big company car and went to see the centre of Stuttgart. All of them, in fact, had seen the centre of Stuttgart quite a number of times (even the tourist had been twice, the first time to write a hotel review and the second time to do something else), but the family council had prepared a programme and there was no going off it. The tourist did not mind.

They walked to a church – it looked massive and solid, with stone walls darkened by the passage of time, and the tourist was willing to bet that it had been here since the beginning of the thirteenth century. His girlfriend's niece triumphantly pointed to the brass sign next to the church entrance which said that the current building was erected in nineteen sixty-five, on the spot of the original church from the fourteenth century which had been destroyed by the Allied bombers. The tourist overplayed his surprise for the little girl. She looked as pleased as if she had built the new church herself.

On Sunday, his girlfriend's sister and her husband trusted them with their daughter for the whole day to take her on a train trip to Ludwigsburg. The girl's parents and Felix walked them to the station in the little town, helped them purchase the most appropriate train tickets and several times explained to them which trains they were supposed to take and where to get off from them.

Ludwigsburg looked like a smaller version of Versailles and all the other palaces built at the same time which had been trying to look like Versailles. There were lots of square, needlessly spacious inner courtyards with improbably white gravel, gardens, alleys and more or less identical buildings with richly decorated façades which had been housing various fractions of the imperial family and were now housing various museums of things like porcelain and lace.

There was something better at the far end of the park: an open-air museum with miniature houses inhabited by moving figures of various characters from classical fairytales. The little girl had been to the museum about a dozen times but she clearly wanted to do it again and she was disappointed almost to the point of tears when they reached the entrance and discovered that the museum was closed. They could see some of the little houses and the figures frozen around them through the fence. The tourist's girlfriend, who was holding the little girl's hand, looked at him. He looked around and climbed over the fence, and then he helped them to do the same. The little girl was fascinated. The tourist was almost certain that it was the first time the child was climbing over a fence.

The museum was delightfully old-school. There was a squat stone tower with a long blonde plait hanging from a window. (The little girl told him that when one pulls on the plait, Rapunzel shows up in the window, but the mechanism was not working.) There was a sugar house with small windows displaying the figures of two children and an open oven. (The little girl told him that when the museum was open, one could see Hansel and Gretel shove the evil witch into the fire, again and again.) There was a house in the woods with an ornate bed and a wolf with a white nightcap under the covers. (The little girl could not remember what exactly happened to Red Riding Hood, but the tourist was left with the impression that it, too, involved some kind of violence.) Finally, they met a maintenance worker with dirty orange overalls who was pushing a wheelbarrow along the pathways between the fairy tale houses. The three of them fell silent as they expected the maintenance worker to call security, confront them himself or at least ask them what they were doing here, but instead he passed by, pretending to be so focused on the task of pushing his wheelbarrow that he did not notice them. The tourist's girlfriend conjectured that the worker's deal was not quite legal, either.

They did not even need to climb over the fence on the way out as the rotating steel door turned quite freely in the direction needed to exit the museum. The three of them walked out like conquerors and returned to the station to wait for their train.

The next day was Monday, the little girl had to go to school and her parents had to go to work, so the tourist and his girlfriend were left to entertain themselves. They took the train to Ulm and as soon as they got off the train on the central station, he realised that something was wrong.

The city stank. There was a strong smell of fertilizer in the air, abating every once in a while only to return stronger than before. People on the streets either did not notice it (which seemed sinister) or very skilfully pretended not to notice it (which for some reason felt even more sinister). There were a dozen homeless people around the entrance of the station who were chain-smoking and drinking beer and when the tourist and his girlfriend walked by, they all turned to look at them. The city was small but chaotic and there was shapeless scaffolding crawling up the façades of many buildings, inadequately concealed with advertising boards which were dirty, torn in places and bleached by the sun. Bronze statues of gigantic sparrows peeked out from behind the corners, taller than humans, with sharp beaks and empty eyes the size of footballs.

At the centre of the city rose the cathedral with its ominously tall bell tower. The tourist's girlfriend asked him if he preferred to climb to the top of the tower first and then have coffee or have coffee first and then climb to the top of the tower. The tourist replied that he had no intention of climbing to the top of the tower whatsoever. (Frankly, he did not want to have coffee, either, but something stronger.) His girlfriend thought that he was joking. The tourist assured her that he was not. His girlfriend pointed out that the bell tower of the cathedral in Ulm was, more or less, the only reason to visit Ulm at all. The tourist cringed and told her that he had already been to the top of the tower and he had no desire to do it again. Then he forced himself to smile and offered her to go alone while he was waiting for her in a café on the opposite side of the square, but it came out wrong. His girlfriend shrugged and they resumed walking through the stinking city.

On the train back, he was watching the darkening landscape outside, feeling her watching him. They had taken the wrong train which hurtled by the little town where her sister lived at two hundred and fifty kilometres per hour and continued on to the next. They got off the train at the first possible station and she called her sister to come and pick them up with the car. When they finally returned to their house, all of them were a little tense because dinner had been postponed until they returned. The tourist offered to take the dog for a walk, but the hosts assured him that they were going to take care of that themselves. They probably suspected that he would not be able to find the way back to the house.

After dinner, the two of them went up to their room and read their books in silence. The tourist switched off the reading lamp on his side of the bed and closed his eyes. After a while, the light was switched off on the other side as well and he felt the girl huddle close to him in the customary position in which they went to sleep, but he could not sleep. He waited for a while and when he could not wait anymore, he carefully pulled back away from her body in order to turn the other way without waking her up.

The teenager had no friends. If someone had asked him why, he would not have been able to provide an answer – he was definitely not the worst geek in the school (by the way, the worst geeks were best friends with each other), he had average grades, he did reasonably well in individual sports and some of the girls even thought that he did not look so bad. (He knew it from the way they would huddle closer to each other and start talking with feigned casualness whenever he walked by them during breaks.) Nevertheless, he knew that he was missing something – and sometimes, although much more rarely, he was convinced that he had something extra – that caused the others simply to forget to call him when they arranged to meet somewhere after school.

167

The teenager did not mind. When he did go out with schoolmates, he was quickly bored by the necessity of doing the same things over and over again and usually waited for the first socially acceptable moment to go home. Not that there was anything special at home – video games, video cassettes, his mother – but when he was alone, figuring out how to spend time was his own problem, to be solved individually, without the peer pressure of his schoolmates. He had never succeeded as a team player. On the rare occasions in which he thought about his future, he always imagined a lonely profession with a clearly set task that it would be his own personal responsibility to complete properly and on time – writing crime novels, working long shifts in a weather observation facility on a mountaintop, driving a truck on international long haul routes. He hated teamwork. He felt that it was useless to try to convince anyone of anything.

Only this time, there was no way to avoid going with his schoolmates, after their German teacher had organised the summer course in Tubingen for a whole year. Two weeks in a natural speaking environment, during which the students would be staying with local families in order to immerse themselves in German-speaking culture and exercise their communication skills at ease. The horror.

Of course, the teenager's host family turned out to be the lamest one of all. They arrived in the evening and were distributed in various homes all over the city, so that when the class reconvened for the first session in the language school on the next morning, all his schoolmates had a story to tell about their host families – some had gotten drunk with their hosts, others were dazzled by demonstrations of financial and pop cultural standards, yet others were mysteriously hinting at the intriguing start of their relationship with the attractive son (daughter, father, neighbour) of the host family. The teenager had nothing to tell. His host family consisted of a man and a woman, around forty years old, who had no children, ate dinner in complete silence, showed him to his room and went to bed at ten in the evening. The teenager looked around his room – it was simple and anonymous like a room in a hotel –

leafed through a few books from the small library and went to bed as well, as he had nothing else to do.

Tubingen was like a fairytale – steep hills with narrow paved streets and old houses, an imposing castle at the top of the city, a flock of unexpectedly massive swans powering up from the runway of the river like a squadron of freight airplanes – but it was a fairytale from the time before literary treatments had sweetened them beyond recognition. The narrow paved streets were still haunted by the ghosts of filth and misery which had reigned there when citizens did not have access to basic healthcare and hygiene facilities. The old houses were marked with darkened signs detailing historical information that teetered between the tabloid and the insane – here is where Goethe had thrown up; there is where Holderlin had lost it completely and had spent the rest of his life under house arrest on the top floor of some carpenter's home. The swans – which he found so interesting that he had to observe them in secret to avoid the ridicule of his schoolmates – turned out to be rough, brutal creatures, harassing smaller birds for their food and fighting each other until blood was spilled, real thugs of the avian world.

During the day, they visited the language course in a windy building belonging to the medieval university where the only compromise with modern times were the electrical bulbs hanging from the ceiling. (The teacher had been illogically proud when she told them how in earlier times, students were obliged to bring their own candles to light their desks.) In the night, they went to the narrow man-made island where an executioner had planted two rows of trees for the benefit of his fellow citizens – presumably in his free time when he was not executing any of them. They bought alcohol from a supermarket with Middle Eastern clerks, who did not ask for identification documents, took it to the island and allocated themselves on the benches – the better benches where the more popular boys and girls sat, had a view to the old town; the others looked on a row of warehouses.

One evening the teenager sat down on a bench with three girls and awkwardly started a conversation with one of them until the others grasped the situation and walked off in the dusk "to check out the other end of the island." The teenager and the girl who had stayed behind drank in silence for a little while, then she moved closer to him and they started kissing, but everything ended on a very unfortunate note when he was suddenly sick while they were still kissing, although he managed to stand up and walk away from the bench before he had to throw up. After that, he did not summon the courage to go back to the girl and the kiss on the bench remained the high point of the evening.

On the next day the teenager was relieved to find out from the girl that she had also been sick a little later, so that his fault about the premature end of their romance was not that unbearable. The two of them sat together on the bus which took the class on a trip to Rottenburg. Their teacher could not sit still with excitement. She claimed that Rottenburg was one of the four most famous places in Germany which everyone interested in German culture and history, as well as everyone in general, simply had to visit in their lifetime. The teenager pretended to make fun of her like all his schoolmates did, but in fact, made a point to remember the other three places so that he could come back and visit them some other time. He did not like to leave anything unfinished.

Shortly after they arrived in Rottenburg, he felt for the first time a very peculiar sensation which was going to haunt him throughout his life. They were walking along a picturesque old street where each house had an ornate sign bearing the emblem of the art or craft practiced in it, when they reached a fork. The street continued up and to the left, leading to a clock tower, and another street went off down and to the right, leading to a fortified wall. The teenager stopped and stared at the streets. He had the feeling that he had already been here... but no, that was not it – it was rather a feeling that some other him had patiently waited at this same spot, some ghostly twin, and just then he had made the final step to the same spot so that the two of them had merged and become one. He blinked and looked at the fork in the street again, with the dark red house on the corner. And then he remembered – he had seen this very spot, photographed by this very angle, on the page of a wall calendar in the cheap hairdressers where he had been last month. The photograph had had artificially intensified colours – rich cherry for the houses, dark gold for the signs in front, impossible blue for the sky – but it had been taken at precisely this spot where he was standing right now. The teenager tried to tell the girl about this, but he either could not find the right words to express his emotion or the coincidence was not as interesting as he thought, because she was not impressed.

In contrast, she was impressed by the torture museum that they took them to visit later. The teenager could not comprehend why the sight of the old machinery with its black iron and dark wood, designed to inflict pain and death to other human beings, caused such strong emotions in his schoolmates. Most boys reacted with excessive enthusiasm and put themselves between the clamps, the tongs and the blades to be photographed. Some girls reacted with unconvincing horror and announced that they were going to wait outside but then did not. The teenager read the information sign next to every exhibit, looked at it thoroughly and then continued on the next. He did not feel any emotions at all, except for a vague satisfaction when he managed to figure out how one of the more complicated torture mechanisms operated.

The next museum on their programme was the Christmas museum which looked more like a supermarket for Christmas toys and gifts to him. There were wooden dolls, crystal balls, blinking lights, cuckoo clocks, porcelain figurines and all kinds of other things that the teenager could not afford and, in fact, had no one to buy for. His schoolmates threw themselves into the shopping, but the teenager had no brothers or sisters and lived with his mother who was sick and did not get out of bed anymore. They had gotten used to talking about it openly; after her last examination it had transpired that she would probably not live to see Christmas.

Finally, they climbed on the inside of the fortified wall of the medieval city where they walked along a continuous narrow path at rooftop height. Every few metres of the wall were decorated with little signs bearing the names of various people and companies who had sponsored the restoration of the corresponding few metres from the wall. For some reason, many of the names of people and companies were Japanese.

The teenager and the girl fell behind from the group, holding hands. He thought that perhaps they were going to make out. He did not mind making out for a bit. The Christmas museum had nauseated him and when he had seen the Japanese names on the medieval German wall, he had been swamped by an inexplicable sensation of hopelessness. Instead, the girl haltingly explained to him that she valued him very much as a person (which seemed a little exaggerated; before the previous night, when they had kissed on the executioner's island, they had hardly exchanged more than three sentences combined), but right now she could not be with him because there were too many things that she had to clarify to herself first, etc. The teenager told her that everything was alright. At some point in her monologue, she had let go of his hand. He had not felt it happen. The girl looked at him with a mixture of pity, relief and gratitude. The teenager had never seen such an expression and he remembered it. It turned out that it was going to haunt him throughout his life as well. Then the girl hurried on to catch up with the others and he stayed behind, running his hand over the signs on the wall as he walked by.

On the final day of their summer course, they were taken on a trip to Ulm to visit the cathedral. Their teacher had already collected the entrance fee from everyone and the whole group noisily passed through and started climbing up. The stairs were so narrow that they walked in single file and the teenager's face was stuck in the ass of his schoolmate in front. He had no one's face stuck in his ass because he was the last in line. The stone railing of the staircase was worn to a sheen by all the hands which had grabbed it ever since medieval times. After a few turns which took them higher and higher, the teenager thought that they must be nearing the top. He asked his schoolmate in front about it, his schoolmate laughed at him and informed him that they had not even cleared the roof of the main building yet.

The teenager was seized by a growing sense of unease. He did not like stairs, narrow spaces and heights, and right now he was forced to climb up a narrow staircase towards the inexplicably high top of the bell tower. He had no idea how they had built this thing at the time when they had still not considered building toilet facilities in their homes. He had no idea why they had built it, either.

They kept climbing up and a fresh unpleasant sensation joined the roll – something resembling motion sickness which he had so far only experienced in vehicles, probably explained by the fact that the staircase rose in a spiral which his vestibular system interpreted as spinning, as if he had been locked in an architectural centrifuge. But then, a few turns later, the bell tower finally broke through the roof of the cathedral and the teenager was horrified to discover that everything so far had been absolutely nothing compared to what lay ahead.

The staircase twisted up through the cone-shaped bell tower tapering to the top and was cut through with elegant windows reaching down to the stairs on all sides. It was as if he was climbing up a rope ladder made of stone. Through the windows – at his feet – was the whole city which kept turning around him as he was climbing up. His legs began to shake. He had to stop and lean on the wall, but even after he closed his eyes, everything carried on turning behind his eyelids.

His schoolmates happily continued up, screaming in affected horror. For some reason, their voices made him feel even worse. He tried climbing with his eyes closed but he tripped over a step and his heart jumped in his throat, so he had to open them again. He was paralyzed for a minute, then he clumsily turned around and sat down on the cold stone stairs. He could not go on. Somewhere far above him echoed the triumphant voices of the others who must have reached the top already. He had to mobilise himself to get up and start climbing down before they had returned and found him in this condition. He promised himself that he was going to count to one hundred and then get up and go, no matter how he was feeling.

But he was feeling terrible. His legs and hands were shaking. His body was covered in cold sweat which seemed to freeze in the sharp gusts of wind bursting through the windows. His stomach was convulsing as if it was getting ready to betray him.

Fifty-one. He kept his eyes shut and tried not to hear the voices of his schoolmates who sounded like they were bored with the top of the bell tower and were coming down already. Fifty-nine. Actually, it would not have been such a nightmare if he had not been with them, if he had been alone. Seventy-four. If he did not have to talk to anyone. Eighty-two. If he could just look and remember interesting things to tell someone later. Ninety-three. Or even not tell, or even not remember, just travel and look. Ninety-eight. Just go and look. Ninety-nine. Just go.

He stood up and painfully started to go down through the vortex of stairs and roofs and empty space, alone.

24. Terminal

The tourist did not suffer from headaches. He suffered from indigestion and insomnia and he had always suspected that if he went to see a specialist, he would be diagnosed with mild (or not so mild) manic depression (or bipolar disorder, or whatever) – but he never had headaches.

Which is why, when he was overcome by a shockingly strong headache at Stuttgart airport, he was simultaneously amazed by its monstrous intensity and bitterly disappointed with himself and the world as a whole – here is something, then, that he would not be spared from for the rest of his life.

His headache started in the region of his right eye and developed quickly as a shock military operation. While they were standing in the departures hall at the airport – the girl, her sister, her sister's husband and her niece (the dog was left in the car, noiselessly barking from behind the window), dark red spots started swimming in front of his right eye, like he had inadvertently looked straight at the sun through the lens of a camera. He blinked a few times, but instead of going away, the spots increased in size and quickly merged into a single massive red spot, brighter now, which was literally obstructing the view from this eye. The girl asked him what was going on. He replied that he did not know. He really did not know. He gloomily thought that at least he could still see with the other eye which should be sufficient to get him through security and on the plane.

Then a long leave-taking with the girl's relatives was in order. The tourist assured them that he had had a lovely time and he was hoping to see them again very soon. In fact, he was almost certain that they would never meet again. They were, too, judging from the awkward manner in which they parted with him. Studying the slight but insistent pain which had started to form behind the red spot, the tourist half-heartedly wondered if they had sensed the change in his attitude or they had read him correctly from the very first moment. There were tears in the eyes of the girl and her sister when they held each other for the last time. Her niece was holding her father's hand. The tourist was holding his bag.

He definitely had a headache – and not just behind one eye – when they gave their passports and boarding passes to the young man behind the plexiglass wall. They passed through in the spacious section of the airport designed to encourage impulse purchases in the travellers left hanging in the zero-gravity of waiting for their flight, and the girl suggested that they sit down somewhere. Her eyes had cleared from the self-pitying ecstasy of family farewells and now they were frankly alarmed by his condition. The tourist thought that he must really look awful if she had gotten so worried.

They sat on a bench and he tried to rest his head back but he clenched his teeth in pain and his face contorted as he raised his head to its previous position and stayed like this, with his eyes closed. He quietly explained to the girl that he had never experienced such a strong headache before. She told him that she had been having migraines for years and the symptoms that he was describing were pointing to something like this. The tourist wanted to object that in his view, migraine was a phantom affection from the nineteenth century which only existed in literature, but the pain reminded him about itself with a surprise stab through the temples and forced him to shut his mouth.

The girl ordered him to stay put until she found a pharmacy. She returned in a few minutes which the tourist spent holding his head like it was a bomb from an action film, containing two different liquid explosives in contrasting bright colours which must not be mixed no matter what. She had bought the most powerful painkiller which could be purchased without a recipe. The tourist irritably asked her why she did not have a recipe for something more powerful if she had been having migraines for years. The girl wisely decided to leave this question unanswered, giving him two tablets with some water instead. The tourist swallowed them. They sat in silence for a while. He said in a tired voice that she could take a walk around the shops without him if she wanted to. She replied that she did not need to do that. He was still sitting with his eyes closed but he had discovered a position in which he was able to rest his head without it splitting with pain. He heard the girl turning the pages of her book. There was something comforting in that sound.

When they called the passengers for their flight to go to the gate for boarding, his headache seemed to have started to go away.

When they landed in Munich after a preposterously brief domestic flight, his headache had disappeared without a trace. Everything around him seemed fantastically bright and light. The children screaming excitedly in a baggage trolley as their father pushed them around in it seemed to be emitting crystal sounds, perfect as pearls. The aroma of pretzels from a bakery seemed to be a whiff from the furnaces of heaven. The colours of the sweaters in a clothes shop on the other side of the hall were like the hues of renaissance stained glass.

Besides, he already knew exactly what he had to do.

He was careful not to touch the girl while they were walking towards the gate for their next flight. She was bright and clear too, with her white skin and her blue eyes and her shining curly hair, and he imagined the black mark that his hand would leave on her arm, the black mark quickly growing to envelop her body, make her smile wither, cut wrinkles in the corners of her eyes, make her heart go cold. He saw this so clearly that he wondered for a moment if it was not a hallucination, a residual effect of his headache or the powerful painkiller, the dying scream of those brain cells which had perished in the fires of agony.

They landed safely, passed through passport control and walked to the baggage carousel where the girl left him to wait for their bags while she almost ran off to find a toilet. (They had had a large draught beer each in Munich, to celebrate the end of his headache.) The tourist obediently stood next to the baggage carousel and ran a mental inventory of the contents of the bag he carried with himself. As always, he had everything that he needed.

He turned and walked away from the baggage carousel without looking back.

The hotel was in a small resort on a lake with a small island with a picturesque castle in the middle. On the other side of the lake, there were steep mountain slopes, and above them soared the peaks covered in snow.

The tourist arrived late in the evening, went up to his room and had an uninterrupted sleep until early next morning when he woke up in reasonably good spirits. As it often happened, the idea for the hotel review had come in the night. He was going to write it in the voice of the vampire prince who lived in the castle in the middle of the lake, watching the fleeting passions of the guests of the hotel with a mixture of haughtiness and commiseration. Naturally, the annals of the vampire prince would include his own evaluation of the hotel.

He opened the window and looked at the lake which was smooth as glass and deathly quiet at this hour. He did twenty squats, twenty sit-ups and twenty push-ups. He made the bed and closed the window. He took a shower and shaved. He put his underwear, socks and shirt in the laundry bag and put on the only clean clothes that he had left. Later in the day he would go out to buy some new ones.

He went down to the hotel restaurant for breakfast but it was still deserted. The tourist sat down at a table in the back of the restaurant, next to the large panoramic windows with a view of the lake and the castle, facing the entrance so that he would immediately spot the client when she entered the restaurant.

He intended to have breakfast while he was waiting.

The young man would not be missed by anyone. His mother had died a few years before, he had no contact with his father and he had no other close relatives. He had no friends, either, at least in the generally accepted sense. The few people that he was meeting more often would probably retain better impressions and memories of him if they met less often.

He had lived past the age in which men still believe in the existence of the one woman in their lives, without particular commotion – and without meeting one. It looked like he would never reach the age in which men accept the existence of a single woman in their lives once again, even though for a different reason.

He had learned the basic gambits of the game so he did not lack sex in his life, but after an initial interest in his peculiar detachment and technical attitude, his partners either established that he was, in fact, quite boring most of the time (the usual phrasing was something along the lines of "not being able to challenge" them), or could not accept the reality that the young man was clearly left unchanged by them. In the end, he always ended up alone.

He did not find any notable inspiration in his job, either: he wrote advertorials and advertising copy and the only challenge for him was finding the next mask to hide behind. He deeply doubted that any of his colleagues or clients would even notice the absence of his texts. He had no ambitions. He had no interests. He had no future.

Which is why he was sitting in this featureless hotel room where he had just gulped down several glasses of water to swallow twenty-four sleeping pills containing barbiturates (he had discovered them quite by chance in a provincial pharmacy where they were sold freely, along with other drugs which were outdated to the point of illegality, such as cough syrup containing codeine and asthma medicine containing ephedrine), and now he was set on drinking the contents of all the miniature bottles of alcohol that he had found in the minibar.

This was not his first attempt.

His initial choice of a suicide technique was jumping off a bridge or a tall building – it seemed practical, it was completely cost-free and relatively easy to accomplish, as all he had to do was take a step, after which gravity would take care of the rest, and even if he changed his mind on the go, so to speak, it would be too late.

Of course, the obvious problem with this technique was his almost hysterical fear of heights. In order to prepare himself, the young man signed up for a bungee jump, but it was an unspeakable disaster. On the way back, some of the adrenaline junkies attempted to motivate him to try another time, but he was slightly catatonic and they quickly gave up and continued exchanging excited stories about their own extreme experiences. He was the only one on the bus who had not dared to jump.

His second suicide attempt involved a safety razor blade and it was an even more embarrassing failure. The emergency room doctor who had put clamps on his cuts (they were so superficial that they even did not qualify for stitches) explained to him in a bored voice how he was supposed to do it properly next time if he did not want the ambulance team to beat him up for wasting their time in which they could have saved another person who had really needed help. He was left with almost invisible scars that he sometimes stared at for several minutes, but it seemed that there were fewer of them every time.

The young man opened a second tiny bottle of whisky and drank it in two gulps, with no ice. The sound which the liquid made when it passed through the tiny plastic neck of the bottle was a parody of the real gollum-gollum a real bottle made; he started laughing before he had swallowed properly, choked on the whisky and suffered a long fit of coughing, but he had to admit that the unusual paroxysm of amused hypersensitivity was probably caused by the stress of the whole situation and not by any effect of the drugs.

Furthermore, he had to admit – especially after the third bottle which contained vodka (he really hoped to lose consciousness and die before he was forced to drink without ice the bottles of gin, too) – that the drugs had no effect whatsoever. All the symptoms that he had enquired about beforehand – lack of coordination, difficulty thinking, inability to judge distance, drowsiness – were completely absent. He felt a little drunk – exactly as he would have felt anyway if he had just polished off a hundred millilitres of whisky and fifty millilitres of vodka in a few minutes. The young man stood up from the bed in the hotel room to look for the package which had contained the sleeping pills. He had swallowed them in the bathroom and had dropped the empty package in the garbage bin. Perhaps he had to check the expiry date.

The pain cut him without a warning. It was low in the gut and it was so strong that the young man bent over and fell on his knees; so much sweat broke immediately on his face that it started dripping off his eyebrows and the tip of his nose. He was seized with an irresistible urge to throw up, which only a moment later faced powerful opposition in the face of a compelling desire to empty his bowels. He started crawling towards the bathroom. He managed to reach the toilet bowl and bent over it, but after he had spent several seconds in this position, he reached the conclusion that the other problem was more urgent after all, so he clumsily pulled himself up (lack of coordination?), lowered himself on the toilet seat, and only then realised that he had not pulled down his pants (difficulty thinking?). Trying to accomplish that without standing up from the toilet seat, he slumped down off the seat on the bathroom floor (inability to judge distance?) and threw up somewhere in front of himself and definitely not in the toilet bowl. He succeeded in clawing back up before he lost control over his bowels and spent the next few minutes racked by sometimes consecutive but more often simultaneous bouts of emptying the contents of his stomach through the two orifices naturally designed for this purpose.

He was bathed in sweat which was quickly cooling off and he had started to shake and his teeth rattled when he finally decided that it was all over, stood up precariously, leaning on the slick tiles on the wall, and busied himself flushing down the toilet and washing the floor and the walls of the bathroom with the detachable shower head. His eyes were beginning to close uncontrollably (drowsiness), so after a while he gave up on this laborious task and crawled back into the room.

He was woken up by the shrill ringing of the telephone on the nightstand right next to his head. They were calling from reception. It was fifteen minutes to twelve at noon on the following day and they were interested to know if he planned to vacate the room or he wanted to stay in the hotel one more day.

The young man croaked back that he had been planning to vacate the room but he had evidently not succeeded. The young man from reception asked him to repeat that as he had not understood what he wanted to say. The young man in the room painfully cleared his throat and this time replied that he would be down in ten minutes. As usual, he did not have any luggage.

He came upon the website just a few days after he had started researching the internet with the keyword "suicide." It looked too well-designed and maintained to be a hoax.

In the course of the following week, he completed a series of ever longer and more detailed psychological tests in which he had to answer standard questions about himself first ("How many days in the week do you drink more than three units of alcohol?"), and then he had to provide brief accounts of some moments of his life ("Describe what you did during the first three days after your mother passed away"). At the end of the week, they contacted him by e-mail and offered an online consultation with a psychologist for which he had to pay up front, using a card. The young man had never seen a psychologist but the fee seemed reasonable.

He did not see this one, either. They used a standard video chat programme but the psychologist remained anonymous. At the end of the consultation, which lasted about an hour, the young man was given a new password and a contract to agree to before he could continue with the process of application.

The process continued for several more weeks in which he was steadily climbing the hierarchy of the website for assisted suicides. Some days, it all seemed like an unnecessarily complicated game, albeit one that he had to admit was more and more interesting. At other times, he thought that it was all a scam – but he had to admit that it was too complicated to justify anyone making money in this manner.

Finally, however, he received a very brief message (especially in the light of all previous communication) informing him that his order had been accepted. He had to transfer one more sum, this time more substantial, and one of their executives would contact him at some point in the near future to complete the order.

The young man did not hesitate. He had already gone too far.

They met at the airport terminal in the late afternoon. The young man arrived a little early, as he usually did, and walked up the stairs to a café where he looked around and sat down at an empty table. Almost all the tables were empty. One of the few customers – also sitting by him – was an old man with snow-white hair and almost crystalline blue eyes.

The man waited for him to sit down before he stood up and came over to his table. He was unusually tall and gaunt. He was dressed in an immaculate light-gray suit and perfectly shined shoes. His only luggage was an old-fashioned briefcase with combination locks. The man asked for permission to join him and sat down. The waiter carried over his drink – vodka on ice.

The man explained that he usually did not introduce himself with his name. If the young man wished to address him in a particular manner, he was free to use his academic title, which was "doctor." The young man asked him what kind of doctor he was. The man looked at him for a moment. He had a narrow face, large ears and very large teeth. He would have looked like a horse if it was not for his lupine eyes. He was a doctor of philosophy.

He explained that the purpose of their meeting was to look at the young man's decision to end his life for one last time. Yes, naturally, he was aware that the young man had already completed a large number of tests and had consulted a specialist, but in his work he had noticed that sometimes human contact changed some factors in the equation. He asked him if he minded this. The young man did not mind.

They were silent for a while. The young man waved the waiter over to order a drink. The doctor politely accepted his offer to have another one. They were silent again. It seemed that the doctor really intended to literally look at his decision, not to talk about it. He was looking very carefully.

The young man asked him how long he had been doing this job. He did not expect a reply but the doctor surprised him by answering willingly and in sufficient detail. New questions arose from his answer and he proceeded to answer them as well, and when the young man looked up to catch the eye of the waiter once more, the clock on the wall told him that they had been there for nearly an hour. The young man could not remember the last time he had talked with someone for a whole hour without feeling bored or uneasy.

The doctor's job was the most interesting thing that he had heard about in his life. At first glance, it seemed absurd, barbarian, preposterous, yet all his questions were met with comprehensive, logical answers. The website was designed to avoid the possibility of being prosecuted under the laws of any country it was operating in. The customers cooperated with the executives to minimise the probability of attracting the attention of the authorities. The executions were completed as painlessly and effectively as possible and some executives (the doctor was not one of them but he was ready to refer him to a colleague) even accepted the responsibility of dealing with all formalities after the fact – funeral arrangements, notifying the relatives, cancellation of facilities, etc.

The young man asked him how he had started out. The doctor was silent once more, looking at him with his clear eyes. His face seemed to be smiling gently, even when he was not. Then he steepled his long dry fingers, leaned in and started talking more quietly, all the time looking straight into his eyes.

To start with, he said, it was necessary to find another profession which demanded constant movement without prior warning. The executive had to possess an authentic explanation for every trip that he had to take to complete his orders. Naturally, this meant that he had to abandon any notions of a career and social life, at least in the generally accepted sense, as they would interfere with the performance of his duties.

The doctor sat back once again. He looked like he was not in a hurry to go anywhere. The young man glanced at his glass. The ice had melted.

A tourist, he thought.

THE END